D0592339

Elephants in the Living Room, Bears in the Canoe

Elephants in the Living Room, Bears in the Canoe

by

EARL&LIZ HAMMOND

with

ELIZABETH LEVY

DELACORTE PRESS / NEW YORK

PHOTO CREDITS

1, 2, 3, 4, 5, 6, 7, 23, 41, 46, 47, 48, 51, and 52: Photographs by Lee E. Barnes. Copyright © 1974 by GRIT. Reproduced by permission of Grit Publishing Company, Williamsport, Pa. 17701.

10: Photograph by Volney Phifer.

21, 29, 30, 32, 33, and 39: © Olympia Brewing Company 1977.

31, 34, 35, 36, 37, and 38: Lear Levin Productions.

40, 45, and 54: Star Gazette, Elmira.

43: Taken at Citizens & Northern Bank, Tioga, Pa.

Designed by Giorgetta Bell McRee

Library of Congress Cataloging in Publication Data

Hammond, Earl.
Elephants in the living room, bears in the canoe.

1. Animals, legends and stories of.
2. Animals, training of. 3. Wild animals as pets.
I. Hammond, Liz. II. Levy, Elizabeth. III. Title.
QL791.H23   1977   636'.96'1   77-802
ISBN 0-440-02251-7

To those who made it possible—
our animals.

CONTENTS

Elephants in the Living Room, Bears in the Canoe

1

Our Animal Kingdom

In a corner of the basement in a farmhouse in Pennsylvania, Mignon, an elephant, gets out of bed. She is probably the only elephant in the world who routinely sleeps on a bed. It doesn't take her long to get bored with the lack of company, so she lifts her trunk and gives a short trumpet.

Directly above her, Liz and Earl Hammond are asleep. Their blankets are tangled at the bottom of the bed; the house is overheated in order to keep the cellar warm enough for Mignon. Liz hears the trumpet and switches on the light. She stumbles into the kitchen and grabs a half-gallon baby bottle from the drainboard, "Hiya, pussycat, I'm coming," she shouts down the stairs. Mignon rumbles a deep throaty welcome. Grabbing a can of evaporated milk from the cellar wall, Liz makes up Mignon's bottle, mixing a formula that simulates the high fat content of elephant's milk.

As Mignon sucks the large nipple of her bottle, Liz scratches the tiny folds of gray skin around her ears. When Mignon was a baby she had to have a bottle every hour, day and night. The Hammonds got her when she was just two months old and weighed only 150 pounds. Earl could carry her in his arms then. Now she weighs over 2,000 pounds and stands five feet at the shoulder. As she drinks from her bottle, she wraps her trunk around Liz's arm and blows hot air kisses on Liz's face.

"Elephants in the wild often stay close to their mothers all their lives, especially if they are female. They nurse for five or six years. I became Mignon's mommy because I was the one who was with her all the time and she got her bottle from me. Now she is really old enough so that she doesn't need bottles, but I give her a few in the morning and a few in the evening. It's a very strong bond between us, and it gives us time to talk and be together. It's incredible how I find myself talking to Mignon. I tell her my troubles. I even complain about Earl and the kids."

When Mignon finishes her bottle, Liz refills it again and again. After the fourth bottle, Mignon indicates she is through by walking in a circle. Liz takes Mignon's trunk in her hand and blows a kiss in it. Then she gives her one head of lettuce, eight to ten apples, ten onions, ten carrots, five to eight potatoes, three bananas, two giant loaves of Wonder Bread, and a bucket of high protein feed called Zu-Preem Monkey Chow. Next it is time to go upstairs and get breakfast for the children.

As Liz nears the kitchen, she hears a skittering sound on the linoleum. Leonard, the baby Russian wild boar is up, enjoying his half hour of freedom. Leonard belongs to Liz's eleven-year-old daughter Niki. He is allowed out of his cage only when Niki can give him her full attention, and even then he is supposed to be confined to the kitchen.

He darts around with quick staccato movements, holding his head low in the charge position. As he moves, he keeps up a constant barrage of snorting and sniffling noises. He is only four months old and weighs about twenty-five pounds. Everything about him is hard and compact; his hair is bristly to the touch, black with light brown watermelon stripes down his back. These stripes will disappear as he gets older.

As Liz puts on a pot of coffee, Leonard attacks the sole of her boot with his sharp teeth. "Niki! Get him out of here!" demands Liz. It is painfully obvious to Niki that she is the only one in the family to appreciate Leonard. She is trying to prove his usefulness by teaching him to become a "watchboar." Leonard can perform one trick. If Niki raps on the linoleum floor, Leonard will lift his head a fraction of an inch off the floor and scurry over to her. The theory behind the trick is that Leonard will someday hear a burglar and scare him away. Nobody doubts that Leonard can scare away strangers, but Niki seems to have forgotten that most burglars will not knock. After a few practice runs, Niki puts Leonard back in his cage and she and her sister Jenny go off to school.

Later in the morning, Liz fills her pockets with small marshmallows and goes back down to Mignon. Mignon stands by the door to the pen, shaking the chain impatiently. She knows it is time for her walk. As Liz starts to unscrew the lock, Mignon thrusts her trunk in the way. Liz swings the door open and Mignon walks with her past the furnace and up the stairs.

At the entrance to the kitchen, Mignon has to pull in her belly to get through the narrow doorway. In the kitchen she deftly maneuvers herself through the small space between the doorway and the dishwasher. It is a very tight squeeze. Like many old farmhouses, the kitchen has a low ceiling and Mignon looks enormous in it.

Outside in the backyard, Mignon walks slowly, picking up loose ice chunks with her trunk and sucking them in her mouth. She doesn't seem to mind the cold. Elephants are adaptable to extremes in temperature; the only danger is that her ears and tail might get frostbitten. There is not much snow, but the ground is frozen solid and very slippery in spots. Mignon searches out the icy patches so that she can slip and slide on them, her legs go off in all directions, and she seems to enjoy the sensation of dancing the Charleston.

In a small pasture to the left, Moose, the red deer stag star of the Hartford Insurance ads, trots to the fence to receive a marshmallow from Liz's pocket. He turns away as Mignon comes closer. Further up the hill, Liz opens the gate to the pasture. Mignon runs ahead to her favorite pair of trees, which she has bent into an arch so she can comfortably scratch her stomach.

When Mignon was young she always walked with her trunk touching Liz's arm, like a toddler holding onto her mother's hand. Liz and Earl could walk down the streets of New York with Mignon loose between them. However, now that Mignon is older she likes to run ahead and enjoys startling the cows in the pasture.

"I try to take her on a long walk every day," says Liz. "Elephant herds in the wild average twenty to twenty-five miles a day. There are a lot of times when I wish I were part of a herd. Elephants have an 'auntie' system—other females help the mama raise her babies. The teenagers, rather than the mothers, chase the little ones around when they leave the pack and get into trouble. Mignon is just getting into her pre-adolescent independent stage now. I told Earl I wouldn't mind getting a teenage elephant as a care-taker. He turned white. I don't think he is ready for another elephant.

"If I were a real elephant mother and she was being a pain in the neck, I could just pick her up and shake her or give her a powerful swat with my trunk. My problem is that there is nothing I can do to her that is the equivalent of that. I don't ever want to treat her as roughly as some trainers might do. Elephants become dangerous and revengeful if they are handled roughly without good reason. Elephants are unusual in that they will wait and wait to get revenge on someone who has mistreated them. You *do* have to treat them roughly to discipline them. However, you should only discipline them when they do something wrong. They take discipline very well without getting hostile, but some people pound on them all the time. Mignon is spoiled. Nonetheless, we do have an extraordinary amount of control over her. We are the only family she has known. She may run fifty yards in front of me, but at least for now I know she'll stop."

While waiting for Liz to catch up, Mignon swings

her trunk back and forth like a contrite child. Elephants have extraordinarily mobile faces. Their eyes are small, but they can move their trunk in so many ways that it makes their expressions change from moment to moment. When Liz chides Mignon for running ahead, Mignon bumps her head against Liz's stomach, and her trunk snakes up her side and into the pocket of her jacket as she searches for a marshmallow. Liz takes off her gloves and feels the edge of Mignon's ears. They are still soft and pliable, but up in the pasture the wind is cold. "I've often wished someone would invent battery-operated elephant ear warmers," says Liz. "I admit the market would probably be limited to Mignon. I have often thought of trying to use a pair of fluffy toilet seat covers. They'd probably be a perfect fit, but I can't figure out how to keep them on."

After feeling Mignon's ears, Liz decides they both have had enough. On the way back to the house, Mignon moves ahead. Liz grabs her tail and pulls sharply. "Mignon Hammond, you walk like a lady." Inside the house, Mignon gets several minimarshmallows as a treat for being relatively well mannered. Then Liz opens the cellar door and Mignon carefully places her front feet on the steps below her. She steadies herself with her trunk, bends her legs, and bumps her way down the stairs.

By now, Earl has long since been up, had his black coffee, and gone down to the barn about a hundred yards from the house. He does his chores, feeding the wild boar, the wolves, the chimpanzee, the bobcat, the Appaloosa stallion, and then goes to work rebuilding new animal pens. Much later, just before evening, Earl decides to take Sasha for a walk.

Their excursion has none of the carefree air of Liz's walk with Mignon. Sasha is a Kodiak bear. At three years old she weighs over 800 pounds and stands nearly seven feet tall on her hind legs. Her claws are longer by inches than any man's fingers. Each paw is nearly a foot in diameter. Friends and neighbors sometimes join Liz and Mignon on their walks. However, nobody but Earl goes near Sasha when she is out of her cage.

He takes her out of the barn to a fenced-in exercise pasture. As she walks, the sun plays on her golden coat; her coat is thick and each hair is silver-tipped like a grizzly. The thick coat hides the muscles of her 800 pounds. Kodiaks are the world's largest bears and they are extremely strong, capable of knocking down small tree trunks with a single paw swipe. Unlike some circus bears, Sasha's claws and teeth have not been pulled; her paws have not been broken.

"I've seen the results of trainers that break a bear's paws so they are not able to hook, even after the break has healed," explains Earl. "A bear's strength is in its shoulders and back and they can only use that strength when they can throw a hook. Sasha could break a person's neck in one swipe, and my neck is usually the one that's closest to her. But her whole personality would change if she were incapable of hurting me and I love her this way.

"If you can't handle the animal the way it is, then you have no business with it. If you alter an animal by pulling its claws, for example, you've only got the shell of it, you haven't got the animal. Sasha's not tame. I don't think there is any such thing as a tame wild animal. Sasha is willing to have me around her. Sometimes she'll do the things I tell her, but to me, if you say you've tamed an animal, it means you've turned the animal into something whose behavior you can predict. I can't predict what Sasha will do. I can't predict Liz or the kids. Sasha's not a windup toy. She's a wild animal. I don't control her."

As they walk in the pasture, Sasha digs in the ground with her long claws. It has started to snow. She shakes from side to side in pleasure, sticking out her long tongue to catch the snowflakes. Earl ruffles the fur on top of her head. "Oh my . . . don't you like the snow . . . Daddy's such a meany because we have to go back." He leans over, snaps a rope around her neck, and leads her back to the barn.

At the barn door, Sasha shifts her weight onto her back legs. In an almost imperceptibly quick movement, she swipes at Earl with her front paw. She misses his leg by a fraction of an inch. "No!" Earl shouts, rapping her sharply on the nose. Sasha puts her paw down and shakes her head vigorously. "She wasn't trying to hurt me just then," says Earl. "She just wanted to remind me she is boss, but it shows you how unpredictable she can be. In many ways, I'd rather work with three tigers than a bear. A tiger can be aggressive, but you can see it coming. A bear changes in a flash, from one moment to the next. They are cunning and that makes them fun to work with, but they are so darn unpredictable. Perhaps I'm the same way."

Sasha returns to her cage without further incident.

Earl gives her a dozen carrots, a dozen apples, two loaves of bread, two pounds of smelt, and six to eight quarts of dry dog food. After feeding her, he checks to make sure that the other animals in the barn are all right. He takes a can of soda out of a cooler and hands it to the chimpanzee, Donna Rae. It's her evening treat. Then he leaves the barn, turning out the lights as he goes. It is dark as he walks up the hill to the house.

Liz and Earl Hammond's farm is not a zoo; it is not open to the public. It is a working farm. On their 500 acres, the Hammonds and their children combine farming with animal training. They call their company Animal Kingdom Talent Services, Inc. Mignon, Sasha, Moose, and others are available for commercials, movies, and educational programs.

The elephant and the bear are only the stars of the kingdom. The supporting cast includes a bobcat, a chimpanzee, a herd of Appaloosa horses, fifty head of cattle, a dozen wild boars, a llama, a baby jaguar, and a lion cub. Liz and Earl bring completely different backgrounds to their marriage and to their work with animals, but together they have created an animal kingdom where a lion actually shares a bed with an elephant; where the deer and horses, the cows and the elephant play; where the humans work very hard and sometimes go quietly crazy watching their dream come true.

How to Acquire
an Elephant

Earl would like to point out that having an elephant as a house pet was never part of his dream. He dreamed of sharing his life with bears, bobcats, owls, and falcons, but never elephants. He insists that elephants would have played no part in his life if he hadn't met Liz.

Liz admits that this is true, but argues that her dream would not have come true if she hadn't met Earl. It is unlikely that another man would have shared his living room with an elephant. The decision to raise a baby elephant was not entirely whimsical. Between them Liz and Earl had decades of experience as animal trainers. Moreover, at the time they acquired Mignon they had a unique landlord, a man who knew as much about elephants as any man alive.

In 1972 the Hammonds were living at Volney Phifer's twenty-seven-acre farm and roadside zoo in New Jersey. Liz and Earl were supporting themselves by traveling around the country with a small petting zoo, but home base was Volney's farm in New Jersey. Volney was a widower in his seventies who had been one of the first animal trainers in motion pictures. He had owned and trained Leo, the MGM lion, and worked for years on MGM movies including *The Wizard of Oz* and *The Good Earth*. He had experience with every aspect of the animal business. He was born right in a circus. His family had been in circuses since the 1700s. His father trained elephants and bears; his mother worked in the center ring with twelve lions.

Liz and Earl rented Volney's farmhouse and helped take care of Volney's extraordinary collection of animals. He had an assortment of rare birds, snakes, alligators, and crocodiles; a pair of toothless old lions, compatriots of Leo; several wolves; baboons; a yak; an African porcupine; badgers; racoons and dozens of rabbits and chickens, as well as a small herd of deer and several llamas. The eclectic nature of his collection was partially explained by the fact that Volney ran something of a retirement home for old animals from circuses and traveling road shows.

In the spring of 1972, a man from Coney Island called Liz and Earl and asked if they would be interested in running a small zoo for children at Coney Island for the summer. On a cold rainy day, Liz and Earl drove out to Coney Island. Shivering under the piers by the beach, they were appalled by the site. "It looked like a recycling center run by juvenile delinquents," says Liz. "It was full of broken bottles and decayed cement blocks. It was an impossibly dangerous area for both children and animals, and we saw at a glance it would be backbreaking work to clean it up.

"Earl and I were ready to tell the man to forget it, but he was a real showman and he obviously wanted us badly. There was something about him we liked. I'm not sure exactly at what point the idea came to me, but I took Earl aside and said, 'Let's tell him we'll do it, *if* he'll buy us an elephant.'

" 'What!?' exclaimed Earl.

" 'We'll tell him a baby elephant will be a terrific draw for the petting zoo, but he'll have to pay for it.' "

In one of the more unusual business contracts two lawyers have ever hammered out, the owner agreed to buy an elephant to be owned by Liz and Earl if they would clean up the site and bring their petting zoo to Coney Island for the summer. At that time their zoo consisted mostly of extremely tame barnyard animals whom Liz and Earl knew could be trusted around children. There was a little Tibetan miniature pony, Donna Rae the chimpanzee, and several beautiful whitetail deer.

As soon as Volney heard about their unusual contract, he called his many friends in the animal business and told them to keep their eye out for a good baby elephant. In May, Bill Chase, an animal importer from Florida, called to say he had received a shipment from Thailand that included a two-month-old female elephant.

On May 31, Liz, Volney, and Jenny, who was then five years old, left New Jersey in a Volkswagen bus to pick up an elephant. Earl stayed behind to take care of Niki, business, and the animals. It was raining as they drove down the dreary New Jersey turnpike. While Liz and Jenny slept in the back of the bus, Volney drove through the night. The next day, Liz took the wheel. It took just thirty hours to reach Florida, and they arrived at the animal compound at 1:30 in the morning.

"No one was there," Liz recalls. "I was so disappointed. I wanted to see her right away. We found a motel and took a double room. In spite of our excitement we all fell asleep out of exhaustion.

"Six hours later, I saw her for the first time. It was unforgettable. I had never seen an elephant that little. She was tiny and skinny and very cute. She was no bigger than a large greyhound, about three feet tall, and she had long, wiry hair all over her that surprised me so because it was soft. I opened the door to her pen and went in. Volney tried to stop me. He was always accusing me of rushing in to mother an animal. He wanted me to go have a cup of coffee and talk to his friend. 'Leave her alone,' he said. 'She needs time to be by herself.' I understood what he was saying, but I could not leave her. I sat in the corner of her pen and talked to her softly. I didn't touch her. Her trunk was tiny. It was like a wet noodle with no power in it at all. After a while she came over and sniffed me. Her trunk just dangled limply, but I could feel her warm breath. I sat there for nearly five hours. I did not eat breakfast or lunch.

"When it came time to leave, Volney and I had a fight. I wanted to put her in the back of the bus uncrated. I planned on sitting with her. I felt she had been cooped up in a crate long enough during her flight from Thailand. But Volney felt it would be dangerous to ride with her uncrated, and he would not let me leave unless I put her back in the box. We loaded the crate into the bus. Jenny, my five-year-old daughter, lay on top of the crate with her fingers dangling through the slats. She wanted the baby elephant to know it wasn't alone. Every once in a while Mignon's head would rub against Jenny's fingers. It got hot and uncomfortable on top of the crate, but Jenny wouldn't leave.

"We drove all night. Nobody slept. In the morning we pulled into a small roadside park for a rest. I wanted to get her out of the crate so she could have a little exercise and some food. We opened the end of the crate, and she came barreling out. She slipped out of my hands before I knew what was happening. I couldn't believe her short legs could move so fast. I ran after her and grabbed onto her. Tiny though she was, trying to hold onto her was like trying to hold onto the tail end of a runaway horse. I yelled to Volney to get me one of the large baby bottles we had brought. He did, and as soon as she saw it, she came to me and started to suck on it. Then she calmed down.

"Dr. James Dorney, our veterinarian, had helped me figure out the right mixture of evaporated milk and water to feed her. Elephant's milk is exceedingly rich; it contains 100 times more albumin than cow's milk. Because of that, it used to be extremely difficult to raise baby elephants in captivity. There is a story that the King of Burma once received a semi-albino orphaned elephant. White elephants are sacred. The king ordered relay teams of twenty-four women to nurse the elephant from their breasts for five years.

"In Volney's day, the formula for baby elephants used to be one gallon of raw cow's milk, half a pint of heavy cream, the yolks of twenty-four eggs, and four pounds of overboiled rice, but the invention of high-fat evaporated milk enabled us to use a formula of three cans to a half-gallon bottle and fill the rest with water. We included an additive of lixotonic, a fantastic vitamin supplement, and neocalglucon, liquid calcium, and she thrived on it.

"By the time we took our second break on the way home, I think Mignon had begun to identify me as the one with the food. I could get her to follow me by holding the baby bottle in front of her. Nonetheless, every time we took her out, I was concerned that somehow I'd lose her. I was very grateful when we got home."

At the sound of the Volkswagen pulling into the drive, Earl and Niki came running out. Liz opened the door to the crate and Mignon stepped out. Earl knelt beside her, running his fingers along the crease where her ears met her shoulder. He seemed to find her "tickle" spots instinctively, and Mignon's body wiggled with pleasure.

Together, Liz and Earl led Mignon to the house. Their apartment at Volney's was up five rickety open-backed porch steps. Earl held onto Mignon's ear lightly. He walked up the first step and applied pressure to the ear to show her she was to follow. Mignon's legs locked at the knee joints, and she shook her head from side to side. Liz joined Earl on the first step and dangled a baby bottle in front of her. Mignon began to tremble. It was clear that the steps frightened her, and she could not figure out how to climb them. Liz and Earl exchanged a glance. Then Earl picked Mignon up in his arms and carried her into her new home.

"I'll remember that moment for the rest of my

life," says Liz. "She didn't struggle; she just nestled in with her trunk lying on his forearm. She was so small that without real effort, Earl could lift her up and carry her up the steps."

When Earl was a boy, his parents did not believe in allowing animals in the house as pets. Earl was born into the animal business. Animals were part of their working life, a responsibility, not fun. The house was to be kept clean, a sanctuary from the mess and the anxieties of the workaday world. Earl could not understand this attitude. "I just can't remember a time when I didn't want an animal as a special pet. I was always getting in trouble for sneaking animals into my room, but never in my wildest dreams did I think of sneaking an elephant into the house."

Earl was four months old when he made his first public appearance in the Ice Capades, in a dogsled driven by his father. His father had spent years exploring Alaska, and then toured across the United States lecturing about the Arctic and demonstrating the use of the dogsled. He traveled with a menagerie of animals from the north. Besides the dogs he had several reindeer and an assortment of bears. He met Volney Phifer when he was hired as a consultant to the MGM movie *Eskimo*, and the two men became good friends. The Hammonds' home base was Aurora, Nebraska, but the whole family often helped out on the tours. Earl was taught to drive a dogsled when he was only five. "I was always getting in trouble because I figured you were supposed to fool around with animals and have fun. Father, in turn, always kept his distance from animals. He knew a tremendous amount, and he took wonderful care of his animals, but he kept his distance. I was different. I loved my father's bears. We had several black bears and a polar bear. Sometimes father would stake a young black bear out on a chain, and I would curl up with it for a nap. The other bears were cage animals, and you couldn't really get close to them."

Liz's upbringing was similar in that her parents also did not particularly care for animals in the house. In almost every other respect, their backgrounds could not be more different. Liz grew up in a New York apartment on Manhattan's West Side. Her father was a professor of the economics of transportation at New York University, but that was only one of many interests. He occasionally taught courses in philosophy and Brazilian literature. Liz had spent several years in Brazil when she was a child while her father taught at a university there. In his spare time, William Leonard Grossman was an avid jazz fan, and even found the time and energy to coauthor an encyclopedia of jazz. Liz's mother, Mignon Grossman, was an artist and pianist. They were a family of wide and varied interests, but the spectrum did not include animals and animals were practically Liz's only interest. In order to placate her, her parents bought her a French poodle, but the dog promptly attached itself to Liz's mother and ignored Liz.

Liz's desire to be with animals had to be satisfied with frequent visits to the zoo, and at an early age she became fascinated by elephants. Every Sunday her father would take her to the Bronx Zoo where he spent dollar after dollar for Liz to ride around and around on the elephant.

"When I was about eight, I told him that I wanted

to have my own elephant when I grew up. I remember he looked me in the eyes and told me very seriously, 'There are enough disappointments in life without setting your hopes on things that can never happen. There are certain things that can never be.' "

When Liz was twenty she read an article in a newspaper about an agency that trained animals for television and theatrical performances. After badgering them for a job for months, she was finally hired. One of her first jobs was to supervise Pal, a pinto horse appearing in *La Périchole* at the Metropolitan Opera House. In the first act Cyril Ritchard rode Pal onstage. Liz was dressed as a Peruvian peasant girl, and she stood beside Ritchard to take the reins from him. Unfortunately, Ritchard often forgot to drop the reins. Holding onto them, he would make a dramatic gesture, flinging his arms wide in song. Pal was neck-reined and he would respond to the pressure by backing up into the chorus. At this point, Ritchard would sing out, "Take him . . . take him."

Volney was an associate of the animal talent agency where Liz worked, and Liz became a glutton for his stories about animals. "Many people thought I was obsessed with my work, but I believe it was a healthy obsession. Suddenly I knew what I wanted to do with my life, but there was so much for me to learn. Volney was an encyclopedia of knowledge. When he invited me to rent an apartment at his farm, I jumped at the chance. I had been married, but I had gotten divorced, and I had two small children to take care of. I felt we would all be better off in the country."

A few days before Christmas in 1968, Earl Hammond arrived at Volney's farm. He was traveling around the country with his small petting zoo, and he had met Volney once through his father. On the day Earl arrived, Liz was in bed with the flu. "It wasn't the mild variety," she recalls. "It was the type that makes you feel like your head is in a glass box. I was upstairs in bed when suddenly I heard a booming laugh from the living room. Later I learned that the laugh belonged to a son of Volney's good friend from Nebraska. I was eager to meet someone my own age who also loved animals, but I just felt too sick to get out of bed."

Meanwhile, Earl sat downstairs, visiting with Volney. He had planned to stay only an hour or two, but he stayed on and on. Looking back, he cannot explain his behavior.

"Somehow I knew I couldn't leave until I met the woman who was sick upstairs. It was like ESP, and Liz and I do have strong ESP between us. I had a booking at a shopping mall for the zoo, and I should have been on my way, but I stayed until I could meet Liz. She had a wonderful smile and laugh, even when she was sick."

Liz and the children saw Earl on and off for almost a year, joining him on tour with the petting zoo whenever they could. The petting zoo was a lot of work for Earl and Liz, but it was pure holiday for Niki and Jenny. The star of the petting zoo was a chimpanzee, Donna Rae. "I got Donna when she was just two years old," says Earl, "and she and I got along immediately. Something in the chemistry between us was just right. I could talk to her in a conversational tone of voice, and she would know exactly what I wanted. There was nothing she wouldn't try if I asked her. She learned to roller-skate and to take tickets at the gate. She helped me keep the other animals in line. Traveling with the petting zoo became a lot more fun once she was along. Often if I was alone, I would take her in the front seat of the cab with me to keep me company."

Donna became extremely fond of Jenny, and the two became inseparable when they toured together. Donna had a tricycle and Earl would give both Donna and Jenny a quarter and send them off for ice cream. "Donna would peddle, holding the quarter in her teeth," recalls Liz, "and Jenny would stand on the bar behind the two wheels, hanging onto Donna's waist. They would go to the concession stand and buy their ice cream, but they always had a problem coming back.

"Donna did not want to peddle because she had her ice cream, and Jenny wanted to eat her ice cream, too. But neither of them felt comfortable being away from us too long. Jenny knew that she had to stay with Donna and couldn't run off and leave her. So, coming back, Jenny would be peddling, holding her ice cream cone in one hand and steering all cockeyed. Donna would be on the back, eating her cone. Sometimes the indoor shopping malls would be two or three blocks long, and they would have to go the whole distance. Other times, Jenny and Donna would go off without the tricycle, and they'd hold hands, looking very serious. They were both about the same size at the time."

As they spent more and more time together, Liz and Earl realized they had never been so happy, and after a year Liz convinced Earl to come live with her and the children at Volney's. "Before I found Earl, animals were really more important to me than people," says Liz, and Earl believes the same was true for him. "Even in my closest relationships, there was an almost constant friction because I wanted to be around animals. With Earl that friction was gone. Our mutual interest meant that we wouldn't have to be fighting all our lives. We'd be able to share what interested us."

In 1970, Liz and Earl established their own company, Animal Kingdom Talent Services, Inc. They hoped to get television and commercial work, but their main income-producing activity was still working in shopping centers with animal displays. Neither of them liked being on the road; the children were now in school, and they all preferred to stay at the farm, so they sought work as close to New York City as they could.

For his part, Volney enjoyed having Earl, an experienced animal man, available to help with the chores. Perhaps even more, he enjoyed having a new audience. Late at night, when the children were asleep, Earl, Volney, and Liz would swap animal stories. Invariably, Volney would turn the talk to elephants. "Volney was not a sentimental man," says Liz. "He was very tough, but he had a soft spot in his heart for elephants. He had studied them in India and Africa. He personally knew practically every elephant in the United States and every elephant keeper. During the 1920s he had worked as an elephant troubleshooter for circuses. There were hundreds of little circuses in those days and almost each one had an elephant. Whenever one would run amok, the circus would send a telegram to Volney, and he would go round them up. Of course, he had been raised with elephants. His father had been an elephant trainer."

Every time a circus came to New Jersey, Volney would take Earl, Liz, and the children for a visit. No matter how small the circus was, Volney always knew someone from the old days. One day he took them to meet one of his favorite elephants, Anna Mae, an old cow elephant in her seventies. Volney had once worked with Anna Mae, and he told Liz and Earl that she was one of the special ones—particularly wise and gentle. She could be trusted to stand unstaked in the menagerie, with just a little rope separating her from the crowd.

Holding Jenny in her arms, Liz stood watching Anna Mae in the menagerie while Earl and Volney went to talk to the lion trainer. Suddenly a little boy ran beneath the rope and began to tweak and poke at Anna Mae, grabbing her trunk and pulling it as if it were a bell rope. Liz was horrified; she had heard many stories about circus elephants seriously injuring or even killing people. She did not know whether to dash in and try to grab the boy or to stand quietly. All her training with animals told her to proceed quietly. Anna Mae circled the boy with her trunk. Liz held her breath, fearing Anna Mae might pick the boy up and hurt him. Anna Mae looked around as if wondering what to do. Then she deliberately pushed the boy back into the arms of his mother. She had picked the mother out of a crowd of 200 people.

"It just freaked me out," says Liz. "It was as if Anna Mae were saying, 'He's your child, lady, take

care of him.' I told Volney and Earl about it, and
Volney was not surprised. It is not at all unusual for
an elephant to have extrasensory perception about
people.

"Anna Mae made an indelible impression on me.
She brought back all my childhood fantasies of wanting an elephant. The next morning I woke up at four
and took her a bag of carrots and apples. I fed them
to her and talked to her. I had never forgotten my
early affinity for elephants, but it had ceased to be an
obsession. Now as I stood in the dark talking to Anna
Mae, I knew that someday I just had to have my own
elephant.

"I talked to Earl and Volney about it. Volney knew
the owner of the circus and spoke to him about re-
tiring Anna Mae to our farm. She had only a few
years left to her, and her handlers were just a bunch
of drunken roustabouts or careless kids.

"Unfortunately, as old as she was, Anna Mae was
still a prime attraction for the circus. Circus elephants
are so valuable and expensive to replace that there is
a great temptation to work them until they die. I was
heartbroken that the owner wouldn't retire her.

"A couple of months later, we got a phone call.
Anna Mae was dead. Her handler had forgotten to
lock the door of her trailer securely, and she had fallen
out onto the highway."

Depressed by Anna Mae's death, Liz began to talk
seriously to Earl about the feasibility of getting their
own baby elephant. She told him that if they invested
in a baby elephant they would get enough bookings
in the New York area to enable them to stay at home.
She was convinced that a baby elephant would be in

great demand for commercials and promotional campaigns.

Volney joined in the discussions. In his travels through India, Volney had met several elephants raised from infancy by human families. Invariably, these elephants turned into gentle, trustworthy creatures. In fact, the maharajas' ceremonial elephants were often raised by families. The maharajas would arrange for captured baby elephants to be given to an elephant handler's, or mahout's, family. Because it is so hot in India, both family and elephant lived in an open-sided shelter. The young baby elephant could come and go freely. There was only a dirt floor, so housebreaking was not a serious problem. Elephants raised in this environment were used in intricate parade work for the maharaja because there was little danger that they would trample a human being. Volney said that the elephants he knew in India that had been raised in this manner were the brightest animals he had ever met and often the healthiest.

When Volney had worked in the business of importing animals for zoos, circuses, and movies, he had been deeply distressed because so many imported baby elephants died, either in transit or during their first year in this country. Even in the 1970s there was a 50 percent mortality rate of young imported elephants. It did not seem to matter whether the elephant went to a zoo or a circus, they frequently sickened and died within months in either environment. Volney believed that young elephants needed strong family ties in order to survive. He felt that the best way to insure the survival of young elephants was to make them part of a family.

Earl admitted that in theory it would be a fascinating experiment in animal behavior to raise a baby elephant. Because Liz was so enthusiastic he didn't want to flatly say no, and he admits the *idea* intrigued him. "I never thought it would be a reality." The overwhelming obstacle was money. Liz and Earl had high expenses and very little savings. Earl felt safe in telling Liz that she could have an elephant because he didn't believe they would ever be in a position to afford one, as they usually cost several thousand dollars. "I should have known better," he says in retrospect. "Once Liz gets her heart set on something, the craziest things start happening. . . . We even run into businessmen who agree to buy us an elephant."

On June 4, 1972, around four o'clock in the afternoon, Earl carried Liz's new elephant up the stairs into their living room. Mignon was about to become the first elephant in the world to be raised as a member of a household, in a farmhouse in New Jersey.

3

Living with a Baby Elephant

Mignon seemed bewildered by her new living quarters. She was quiet and subdued for the first few hours, showing very little curiosity. Occasionally she would sniff a chair or the sofa, or stare at the television. Liz felt it was as if she were trying to figure out what was real and alive, and what wasn't. She did not cry or make any noises.

The other animals in the house did nothing to make her feel welcome. Liz's greyhound, Dog, tried to pretend she wasn't there. The two cats were terrified. Robert the bobcat took an instant dislike to her. He hissed and jumped up to the mantelpiece and stayed there.

Niki and Jenny, on the other hand, were overjoyed to have Mignon in the house. Niki showed her around the house, naming everything: "This is the TV . . . this is the kitchen . . . I'm Niki."

"The kids treated her from the beginning as if she

were a foreign child we had adopted who did not speak English, and it was probably the perfect approach.

"Earl and I sat on the couch, staring at her. We could not believe we had really done it. We talked in whispers. I was not at all sure we hadn't taken in more than we could handle. Then, while I was giving her her first bottle in the house, my hand slipped into her mouth, and she began to suck on my thumb. I could feel her muscles relax as she sucked, and I realized I had stumbled on a gesture that comforted her. I kept my hand there for nearly half an hour. I think it was the start of my becoming 'Mommy.'

"I decided to name her Mignon, after my mother. She was very ladylike and delicate. Then, too, I wanted to placate my mother. I had mentioned to her very casually that Earl and I were exploring the possibility of raising an elephant in the house, and she became quite upset. She was convinced her grandchildren would be trampled, and that I was crazy.

"I hadn't told my parents that we were definitely getting an elephant. I thought it would be better to just present them with a *fait accompli*. That first afternoon, I called my parents and my father answered the phone. Mignon stood by my side, drinking a bottle. I had discovered on the trip that if I took the bottle away from her before she was finished she would trumpet, so with my father on the phone, I pulled the bottle out of her mouth, and she trumpeted right into the mouthpiece.

" 'What's that?' my father asked.

" 'That's my elephant in the living room,' I replied. After he got over the shock, he said, 'I will never again say to you that there are certain things that can never be.'

"My mother was too surprised to react. I told her I was naming it after her, and I think she managed a quiet, 'I guess that's nice . . .' but I knew she was upset. She asked me what I was going to do about housebreaking an elephant. She was sure that even if Niki and Jenny escaped being trampled, we would all succumb to a rare disease. I reassured her that Earl and I would never have brought an elephant in the house unless we were sure we could housebreak it, but I was lying."

While Liz was talking to her parents, Earl took up all the rugs and laid plastic matting on the floor. The truth was that neither of them had any idea about how to go about housebreaking an elephant. All the experts, including Volney, said that elephants could not be housebroken, that they simply did not have the muscular control; but after her experience with Pal and the other horses whom she had trained to control themselves while on stage, Liz was convinced that it could be done.

However, the first afternoon with Mignon shook her confidence. "Elephants give torrents. Horses are dainty compared to elephants. I could not believe the amount of liquid coming from that tiny animal. I was too exhausted on the first day to do anything more than just mop it up. It was like living with a dam that burst unpredictably every few hours."

By early evening, Liz was ready for bed. She and Volney had slept little in four days. She tucked Niki and Jenny in bed went out to the living room to say good night to Mignon, for she and Earl had decided that the living room would be Mignon's room. Liz gave Mignon a final bottle, and then she and Earl walked into their bedroom. As soon as they had closed the door, they heard a piercing cry. Liz grabbed Earl and ran into the living room. Mignon was walking around the room in circles, obviously frantic at the thought of being left alone. Earl and Liz exchanged glances. "I went and got our blankets and made up the sofa bed. I told Earl to think of it as an adventure. We were the only people in the United States sleeping with an elephant. Of course, neither of us slept very well that night. Every time Mignon moved we heard her, and every time she urinated, there would be a loud rush of falling water.

"In the morning, I figured out that a bucket was the only answer. I never bothered to housebreak her for defecating because it came out like a hard lump. Wherever she did it, it wasn't hard to pick up. It was the urinating that was the problem.

"My only object at first was to get the bucket underneath her just to contain it. Then I realized she might eventually learn to connect the two in her mind, the way a child is toilet-trained. However, in order to accomplish this, I had to be consistent. I had to be sure that whenever she urinated, the bucket was always underneath her.

"I did not want to yell at her the way I had yelled at Pal. She was such a baby I didn't want to raise my voice to her. My first job was to gain her confidence and trust. I could not scream at her, 'No, No, No!' the way you would do a puppy; she was too sensitive."

In order to be consistent, Liz had to watch Mignon like a hawk. At the moment Mignon began to urinate,

Liz had to rush to get the bucket under her. In order for the training to work, Mignon could not be left alone at night. If she were allowed to urinate freely at night, she would never make the connection. Liz talked Earl into sleeping in the living room. She convinced him that as soon as Mignon was housebroken they would return to their own bedroom.

Liz got very little sleep those first few weeks. Mignon slept on a plastic pad beside the sofa bed. Elephants do not urinate lying down, and so every time Mignon needed to relieve herself, Liz would hear the scrambling, scratching noise of Mignon waking up and scrambling on the plastic mats. She conditioned herself to wake up at that sound and run to place the bucket under Mignon.

"Liz doesn't wear too many clothes when she goes to bed," says Earl, recalling the first few weeks with Mignon. "I'd sleep on the inside, and she'd sleep on the outside. Whenever Liz thought she heard Mignon moving, she'd bound out of bed. So there I'd be, lying there watching Liz chasing an elephant around with a bucket, and watching Mignon trying to avoid the crazy naked lady chasing after her. Mignon would run around getting set to let go, and Liz would be in hot pursuit trying to get the bucket under her. It was the funniest thing I ever saw, and I figured one week of this and Mignon would be in the barn and we'd all get to sleep."

"Earl makes the nights sound like a comic opera, but they had a fairy-tale quality for me. The first few weeks were a time of total wonderment and involvement, especially at night. Everybody was asleep, and it would be nice and quiet, and we would be alone.

After she had relieved herself in the bucket, I would stay awake and play with her. I began to teach her little tricks. We learned about each other. I taught her to pick up her different feet. She learned to put her foot on my face and not press down. She was so little you could pick up her feet and just say, 'good girl.' She seemed to understand my words. I always spoke in complete sentences. Technically, when you are training an animal, you are always supposed to use just one word for each command. I never had to do that with Mignon. If I want her to sit, I have about ten different ways of saying it, and she understands.

"In our late night sessions, I would try to teach her how to use her trunk. It was a floppy little thing, and she had no idea how to use it. A baby elephant cannot use its trunk to drink water or feed itself. Watching a baby elephant learning to control its trunk is very comical."

An elephant's trunk is made up of over 29,000 muscles, each controlled by a different nerve ending. Experts believe that a large proportion of an elephant's brain is devoted exclusively to controlling its trunk, and its brain is extremely large—eight times the weight of a human brain. (Its body is forty times larger than ours.)

Like all young elephants, Mignon's brain at birth was only 35 percent of the weight it would reach when she became full-grown. An elephant's brain grows slowly, and like humans, elephants have a prolonged period of childhood. Herd life is complex and circumscribed by many rules. An elephant in the wild must learn its place within an intricate web of kinship relations. Mignon's new environment was similar in that she had to learn to relate to a variety of humans, to realize what was acceptable behavior and what was not.

After several weeks, she had learned that the bucket was the proper place to urinate. When she had to urinate, she would wait a few seconds until Liz placed the bucket under her. "Those seconds represented a real triumph for her and me. I was elated, but I needed to find a signal so that she could let me know when she needed to use the bucket. Otherwise, whenever we were in the house, I would not be able to leave her side or stop watching her.

"The hardest part of the training was finding a signal. In the beginning, her trunk was so weak it couldn't pick up an empty bucket. However, by the time a few weeks had passed and she understood the connection, her trunk was strong enough so that it could move small things. I had a fantasy that I'd train her to pick up the bucket and bring it to me, but I finally settled for just having her rattle the handle.

"She picked that up very quickly. I would take her trunk in my hand and wrap it around the bucket, showing her how to shake it. Very quickly, she began shaking it whenever she wanted to urinate. It was as if she wanted to go in the bucket, and so it became natural for her to rattle it. When you are toilet-training a child, there is always that wonderful moment of success when the child tells you it has to go; well, this was exactly like that moment.

"Whenever Mignon rattled her bucket, one of us had to race over to where she was standing and whip the bucket in place behind her. She had enough muscular control to wait nearly a minute, but not much longer, so someone had to get there fast.

"The nights became a problem. After I stopped being so tense that I woke every time the floor mat rustled, I began sleeping soundly and the rattling of her bucket was not enough to wake me. She learned to come over and nudge me with her milk bottle. Then one night she clobbered me over the head with it. It was almost full. I'm grumpy anyhow when I first wake up, and she gave me a black eye. I fought back. I jumped out of bed, screaming and carrying on. I scared her half to death. She ran to the corner of the room, spun around, and squeaked.

"That was the end of her hitting me over the head with the bottle. She would come and stand by the bed, gently waving her bottle back and forth until I sensed her presence and woke up.

"As time went on, Mignon became more and more adept at using her bucket. However, once she was more ambitious than her capabilities would allow. She tried to do it herself. I was in the kitchen cooking, and my guess is that she tried to get my attention and I didn't hear her. I heard a noise and came into the living room. She had put the bucket under herself just where it belonged. Then she must have backed up and stepped on it, flattening it like a pancake. She didn't realize the bucket was squashed and started to urinate. She kept watching the liquid running between her legs and all over the floor. I could tell from the expression on her face that she couldn't understand why it wasn't going into the bucket.

"She stood there with a sheepish look on her face.

It seems to me that her face registers emotion very quickly. It has something to do with the way she holds her trunk. Anyhow, Mignon went into a corner and hid herself. She wouldn't come out for about ten minutes."

Once Mignon became accustomed to the bucket, she seemed to realize that the house was not the place to defecate either, and she would wait to make a bowel movement on her daily walk. Liz distinctly recalls their first walk: "I kept her in the house for three days when we first came back from Florida. I wanted to be confident that we had established a relationship so she would not spook and try to run away. It was a beautiful early June day, and I decided I could not keep her in any longer. Earl was working and I was alone with her. She followed me out the front door and then stopped at the top of the steps. She looked at me as if to ask, 'Where's the guy who carried me up here?'

"I told her she would have to learn to maneuver the steps herself. I held a baby bottle a couple of inches in front of her. She swayed back and forth. Finally, she sat down on her rear end and started to lie on her side. I picked up her forelegs and dropped them over the edge of the step. She squirmed around on her bottom. I stood a couple of steps in front of her. Still sitting down, she edged her bottom over the step and plopped down the first step. I was laughing so hard I nearly cried. She bumped her way down to the bottom. I gave her a big hug and a drink from the baby bottle.

"Coming back, she could not figure out how to climb. She tried putting her forelegs on the first step and hopping with her back feet, but her back feet kept missing. I got behind her and pushed. Somehow or other, we made it to the top. She gave a great sigh, as if she would never try to go outside again. I gave her my thumb to suck."

Niki remembers her first walk with Mignon. "We had only had her about a week, and Mom told me to take her out. I said, 'I don't know how to lead an elephant. I've never had any experience with it.' Mom said, 'Look, you're even. She doesn't have any experience being led; the two of you can learn together.'

"It started out OK. Mignon bumped her way down the stairs. But when we walked over to the barn, she must have known that I wasn't used to anything like this. She turned around and started to split for the house. Fortunately, she couldn't move fast then, and I got ahead of her and stopped her.

"She was different from any other animal we ever had. She could do so much more. I was a little scared of her at the beginning. Mom let Mignon suck her thumb all the time, and I knew she wanted to suck *my* thumb, but I was frightened. I thought she had teeth up there, but it turned out to be very smooth. Soon I learned to let her suck my hand and you could tell she loved it.

"Jenny and I taught her to play kickball—not just to fetch like a dog, but to really play the game. If you rolled a ball to her, she would kick it, and then Jenny or I would kick it back to her and she'd run and get it, set it up with her trunk, and kick it back to us. She picked up on games; you almost did not have to teach her."

A couple of weeks after Mignon's arrival, Liz's parents came out to meet her.

"I was anxious for them to think she was as cute as I thought she was. My parents are quite fussy. My father is especially careful about plates and silverware and what he eats. He wipes off every utensil in a restaurant and cleans it. He's sure bacteria is on everything.

"I decided to cook my specialty, Moroccan lamb stew. It's a very complicated recipe. My parents came early in the afternoon. Mignon was very well-behaved and sweet. My parents walked around her a little gingerly and sat down. Mignon stood a respectable distance away from them, and then suddenly she began to have awful diarrhea. I was mortified. It seemed to confirm my mother's worst nightmares about my life. I had to keep running into the living room and clean up her mess. Then I'd wash my hands and run back and put more food in the pot. My mother got a very bad headache and went out and stayed in the car. My father couldn't decide whether it was horrible or funny.

"That night he proved to me how much he loved me. He ate a big dinner. It absolutely amazed me because I was sure Earl and I and the kids would be the only ones with stomachs that strong. My mother came back in, and she was a terrific sport, too. There we were, sitting around the table trying to be social, and then we'd be interrupted by this loud splattering noise! It was a realistic introduction to our life with Mignon, but it was not the side that I wanted my parents to know about. They left, firm in their opinion that I had made a terrible mistake in getting Mignon, and that I was more than a little bit crazy."

Despite such mishaps, once the housebreaking problem was solved, Liz and Earl discovered that Mignon adapted herself easily to their routines. She was endlessly curious. When Liz cooked, she would follow her into the kitchen and watch each step. Liz likes to experiment in the kitchen and has a collection of over sixty cookbooks, covering nearly every nationality and point of view—everything from *Grandma's Country Cooking* to *Modern French Culinary Art* to *The Naked Chef's Aphrodisiac Cookbook.*

Liz discovered that if she placed a cookbook on the floor next to Mignon, Mignon would riffle through the pages with her trunk in imitation of Liz. A giant encyclopedia of French cooking became one of Mignon's favorite toys.

From the beginning, the television fascinated Mignon. As she became adept at using her trunk, she discovered how to turn the set off and on. She also learned to sit in a chair. She taught herself, choosing an old-fashioned slat rocker. "It wasn't a trick," says Liz. "I think she learned just by watching us sit in chairs. About half of what she learned, as a really small elephant, she learned from watching us. She would turn her back on the rocker and ease her bottom into it. She fell off several times, but she kept trying and succeeded. She looked just like a little fat lady, with her feet up, rocking back and forth, watching television with the family. When she got bored, she'd turn the television off."

"She used to make me mad," recalls Niki. "You'd

be sitting there watching TV, and a good movie would be on. Mignon would get out of her chair and stand right in front of you. If you yelled at her, she'd turn the set off."

Mignon seemed to love music. When the record player was on, she would wave her trunk in rhythm with it and rock her body back and forth. She developed decided tastes in music. She loved the heavy beat of Janis Joplin, but more complicated rock music such as the Jefferson Starship seemed to confuse her. "She loved footstomping music," says Liz. "Janis Joplin was her favorite, and she also loved the Band and the Beatles. She seemed to like individual rock singers more than bands. If you put on a singer who was rhythmic and loud without being a big noise, then she really related to it . . . she really dug it."

In the wild, the very young baby elephant rarely strays more than a few steps from its mother's side. As the herd wanders for miles in search of food, the baby elephant ambles beside its mother, often touching her with its trunk. Within a few weeks of her arrival, Liz began to take Mignon with her as she did her errands around New Jersey. Mignon fit easily into the back of the Volkswagen bus and appeared to love riding. She never got carsick.

"Once I was sure she was housebroken, I could take her everywhere. I could treat her as casually as if I had a well-behaved dog next to me. I'd take her to the shopping mall whenever I had to go there to buy anything. She never got kicked out of a store. People were too astonished. Nobody had ever seen an elephant that little.

"You could see their eyes try to take it in . . . a

trunk . . . it was gray. . . . A few people thought I had a dog in an elephant suit. Sometimes they would treat her roughly because they were sure her trunk and tail were made out of rubber or *papier-mâché*. More than one person wanted to know where her zipper was. They thought she was a person in an elephant suit.

"I had a wonderful time. I took her into B. Altman's to get her a sunbonnet. We tried on lots of them. She never once grabbed at anything or tried to pull things off shelves. She was such a perfect lady that they ended up giving her a wonderful straw hat.

"I used to take her to Newark Airport to pick up Earl. He had to be away fairly often when she was little. They had a big No Pets sign up on the door. One guard tried to stop me. I just asked, 'Who ever heard of an elephant as a pet?' We walked right past him, and the guard stood flabbergasted until we were too far away for him to stop us.

"When she got a little older, Earl and I would take her into New York with us. We'd walk up and down Fifth Avenue and window-shop. She'd walk between us, waving her trunk. She loved the city. Occasionally we would take her into a restaurant like Max's Kansas City or the Buffalo Roadhouse. Mickey Ruskin, the owner of Max's, loved her. He would order her a huge salad and she'd eat it very daintily. A lot of artists hung out at Max's and some of them would pretend to act so cool as if to say, 'Oh, sure, I've been to lots of bars with an elephant before.' "

"It was fun," recalls Earl. "You'd walk down the street, and half the people would just glance and keep right on going, never looking back. Then somebody would walk by, get about fifty feet ahead of us, turn around, scratch his head, and just stare. The funniest reactions were from the people who would spot her, and their eyes would skitter off. Their brains absolutely refused to register that they had seen an elephant."

When they went to the city, Liz and Earl would take Mignon to see Liz's parents. After their initial visit, the Grossmans always seemed to have an excuse not to come to the farm, so Liz and Earl went to them. As the weeks went by, Liz and Earl noticed a subtle difference in Liz's mother. She began answering questions from passersby and acquaintances in the unmistakable tones of a proud grandmother: "Yes, the elephant was housebroken. . . . It was the only elephant in the Western world being raised as a member of a family. . . . It was incredibly gentle with children . . . elephants are very intelligent, with very large brains. Yes, the elephant was named after me."

Mignon had been living with Earl and Liz for about six weeks when they decided they needed a day to themselves. Volney was not available to babysit, so they asked a couple who occasionally worked for Volney to take care of Mignon. They showed the couple how to prepare her baby bottles, how to play with her, and what her favorite toys were. They were exactly like parents making arrangements to leave a new baby for the first time.

Liz drove away with no qualms. She and Earl spent the day in New York City, enjoying their freedom. As far as Liz can remember, she did not worry about Mignon at all. It was late at night by the time they returned. As they approached the house, they heard trumpeting. There was a note of distress in it that Liz had never heard before. Earl braked in front of the house and Liz bolted out of the car and ran up the stairs. She found Mignon trapped in a tiny hallway. A closed child's accordion-gate separated Mignon from the living room. Mignon weighed close to 300 pounds and could have smashed the gate easily, but she had behaved and stayed behind it.

With Mignon following her, Liz stormed into the living room and confronted the couple. "Why was Mignon locked out of the room that was home to her?"

"Oh," the couple replied blandly, "she kept getting in the way while we were trying to watch television." Liz was furious. She threw the couple out, then turned her attention to Mignon. Her first priority was to give her a bottle. Mignon's breath was coming in great heaves; her sides were caved in, outlining her ribs. When baby elephants get frightened and upset, they become dehydrated very quickly.

Earl came in while Mignon was finishing her bottle. Liz asked him to sit in with Mignon while she went to the kitchen to prepare a second bottle. As she turned to go into the kitchen, Mignon tried to follow her. Earl noticed that she walked with a slight list. She was also scratching her ankles, one foot against the other, as if they itched.

Liz tried to feed her a couple of mashed bananas, but she wasn't interested. Earl told her not to worry —Mignon was probably still upset. They went to bed on the couch in the living room. Mignon lay down on her plastic mats and seemed to go off to sleep peacefully.

The next morning, Mignon could hardly walk.

Then she began having convulsions, would scramble to her feet, and then fall. Liz tried to calm her down and to comfort her, but she had a desperate urge to stand, and each fall triggered off a new set of convulsions. Earl called their veterinarian, Dr. James Dorney of the Summit Dog and Cat Hospital in Summit, New Jersey, who told them to bring her right over to his animal hospital. Mignon was too weak to negotiate the steps. Earl picked her up. She struggled in his arms for several seconds, almost causing him to fall. Then she stopped thrashing, as Earl spoke to her, "It's going to be all right, baby love, you're going to be OK, love. . . ."

"I remember watching Earl carry her down the steps. It was like a nightmare. My mind flashed to the very first day we brought her home, when Earl had carried her up the steps. I couldn't bear to think we might lose her."

Liz got in the back of the Volkswagen with Mignon while Earl drove. When they arrived at the animal hospital, Dr. Dorney was waiting for them. Earl carried Mignon into a big room in the back. As Earl and Dr. Dorney spread newspapers on the floor, Liz held Mignon's head, trying to comfort her. Dr. Dorney performed a quick examination.

"I don't know what she got into," he said. "Perhaps it's an infection or it may be poison, but she's having a toxic reaction to something. Let's just hope we find out what it is before she dies."

Before she dies. The words were out, and other words, unbidden and horrifying, came into Liz's mind: *Fifty percent of all baby elephants imported die. . . .* "I had felt so sure that we were doing everything the right way. I was convinced that it couldn't happen to Mignon, that we had provided her with the close family relationship she needed. Now I was not sure of anything. I felt that I had been arrogant. I was heartbroken and helpless.

"The one thing I could cling to was my faith in Dr. Dorney. He was basically a small-animal practitioner, but he was one in a million. When he was younger, he had worked with an animal importer, so he had some experience with exotics. But beyond that, he had compassion and infinite curiosity and a dedication to his work. A lot of local vets won't touch exotics. They tell you to take them to a specialist. Dorney wasn't like that. I knew he'd work like hell to save her."

Hurriedly, Dorney began running tests. Mignon was convulsing badly, and it seemed clear to him that she was close to death—with perhaps no more than ten or twelve hours to live. He placed calls to several elephant experts in zoos around the country and even made a call to a veterinary college in India. All the experts told him the same thing: Once they begin convulsions, it's only a matter of time until they die.

Dorney hung up the phone after the last call and stormed back into the room with Mignon and Liz. "Those sons of bitches," he said. "They're sure she is going to die. I'll do my best to save her. Maybe I'll do more harm than good, but she's going to die anyway if I don't do something. Will you let me experiment?"

"Do whatever you can," said Liz.

Dorney knew he could not give Mignon too much penicillin because elephants are very sensitive to it.

It destroys all the natural bacteria in their stomachs and leaves them prey to several secondary infections. So Dorney began by giving Mignon antihistamines and several of the mycins, and some electrolytes and glucose just to keep her strength up. He had to take blood samples every few hours to know if the medication was having any effect.

There aren't too many places where you can get a needle into an elephant, and it's even more difficult to take blood. The ears are the only place where the veins are close enough to the surface, and an extra wide needle has to be used because an elephant's blood is unusually thick.

In those first few hours, Dr. Dorney could only hope to keep Mignon alive from one moment to the next. Finally, he found two vets, Dr. Marty Dennis and Dr. Berenberg, who were elephant specialists and troubleshooters for zoos and safari parks. They loved elephants, and they were the only ones he consulted who were not completely defeatist. The two had written a medical paper on the subject of elephant's blood, and they were able to tell Dorney what her red and white cell counts should be and which drugs were safe. After he talked to them, Dorney began to feel more confident about his treatment of Mignon.

The day wore on. Mignon got no better, but no worse. Liz asked Earl to bring blankets and pillows. Dorney had told her that the greatest danger was that the infection would sap her will to live. Most baby elephants who get that sick merely stop eating and die.

Earl brought in bunches of bananas. Liz peeled each one, broke it into two-inch segments, and hand-fed them to Mignon. The office began to look like a monkey den.

Liz spent forty-eight hours in the hospital with Mignon, not leaving her except to go to the bathroom. "Those hours are a blur to me. I was so scared she was going to die. She could hardly stand. When she'd fall, I'd try to get my legs under her, because she couldn't get back up herself and that would upset her a lot. If I timed it right, I could position myself so she'd land on my lap, and then I could use my legs as a lever and push her up. But if something other than her side hit me, like her shoulder bone, boy, did I feel it! However, since she was upset if she was not standing, I had to help her stay on her feet. She was terrified of lying down, and it frightened me to see her on her side. She looked like she was dying. I was glad she wanted to be upright. I felt it meant she was putting up a terrific fight for her own life."

After Mignon had survived the first forty-eight hours, Dr. Dorney felt she could go home. The convulsions had stopped. He felt that if she got back to familiar surroundings, she might calm down. The greatest danger now was that she might die of exhaustion. Elephants in the wild have an instinct that tells them to keep standing, no matter how sick they are. It is an instinct that derives from the fact that in the wild, a sick elephant has to keep up with the herd or die. Elephants have been observed supporting a sick elephant between them.

Dr. Dorney believed that Mignon's problem was the reverse of what it would have been in the wild. She needed sleep in order to restore her shattered nerves from the convulsions. She could still easily die from shock. Earl and Liz helped Mignon, wrapped in blankets, into the Volkswagen. Earl drove and Liz sat in the back. Mignon lay on her side, her head resting on Liz's lap. When they got home, Earl carried her up the stairs. Niki and Jenny came up and put their arms around her. She raised her trunk to Jenny's face. "I told her I loved her and that I was so happy she was alive," recalls Jenny. Mignon turned away from the children and tried to reach Liz. She stumbled and fell. Earl went to her and laid a hand on her side. He spoke to her softly, trying to soothe her into lying on her side. She took several deep breaths, and for a moment Earl felt she would rest, perhaps fall asleep. Yet seconds later, her breathing became labored. She struggled to get her feet under her. Earl helped her up.

During the first hour at home, Mignon appeared more agitated than she had at the hospital. She seemed pathetically worried that Liz would leave her. If Liz just got up to go to the kitchen for a baby bottle, Mignon would trumpet weakly and try to follow her. It was as if she had understood that while they were in the hospital, Liz would not leave her; once they were at home, she feared Liz might leave and not come back.

Liz brought a baby bottle from the kitchen and sat down on the couch. Mignon stood by her side sucking from the bottle. Earl sat in the rocker across the room. He watched his wife and Mignon. Mignon looked frail. He had never believed an elephant could look frail, yet she did. It looked to him as if she had lost more than thirty pounds in two days.

Liz looked exhausted, too. Suddenly, Earl had an

idea. He got up, putting a finger to his lip, signaling Liz to be quiet. He tiptoed over to Mignon, then suddenly shoved his weight against Mignon's side. She toppled over onto Liz and Earl's bed. Earl put his hand on Mignon's shoulder and told Liz to do the same. Jenny got a pillow and put it under Mignon's head. Within minutes, Mignon's eyes were closed and she was sound asleep.

"The idea just came to me," says Earl. "I realized that in the six weeks she had been living with us, we had become Mommy and Daddy. We were the symbolic herd, and she had to keep up with us. Well, for six weeks she had watched us sleep in that bed. My guess was that it represented a safe resting place, a place where Mommy and Daddy wouldn't leave her. And it worked."

Liz put her head against Mignon's on the pillow. Earl got a blanket and covered them. They both slept for hours. For the next several days, Liz stayed with Mignon on the bed, constantly feeding her baby bottles and bananas to build up her strength. In less than a week, she was able to stand without shaking.

Now that Mignon was on her feet again, Liz and Earl wanted their bed back, but Mignon refused to sleep on the plastic mats anymore. When Earl got into bed beside Liz, Mignon would try to climb in. When Earl told her to get off, she would stomp around the room in small circles.

"I was not going to sleep with an elephant," said Earl. "Volney had an old mattress. I put it up on a plywood and cinder block base, and took Mignon over to it and explained that it was her bed. She understood me all right; she just didn't like it. The first night, she kept trying to get back into our bed, but every time, I would lead her over to her own. In the middle of the night, Liz got up and put sheets and a pillow on Mignon's bed, and she seemed to like that better. But she never really accepted the idea. I feel she has always believed that she belongs in Liz's bed and I do not. It has been a constant struggle between us.

"I tell you, Liz talks about what a fairy tale that first year was, but we couldn't make love, we couldn't do a goddamn thing without that little elephant interrupting. Mignon would hear us start to make love, and no matter how quiet we tried to be, she'd come bounding out of bed. I'd look up and see that big eyeball coming down on me. Then she'd take her trunk and try to pull me away or off the bed.

"Sometimes when we were asleep, she liked to come over quietly and wrap her trunk around Liz. She'd curl her trunk around Liz's chin. One night, I woke up feeling very loving toward Liz. I rolled over and gave her a peck on the cheek. Only it felt funny. I had kissed that elephant's trunk. I looked up, and I knew she was laughing at me. For a second, I was furious. Then I started to laugh, too."

1 through 5: Mignon climbs cellar stairs into kitchen and discovers Jenny waiting for her.

6   Niki takes a ride on Leonard, the Russian boar.

Liz and Robert Bobcat.

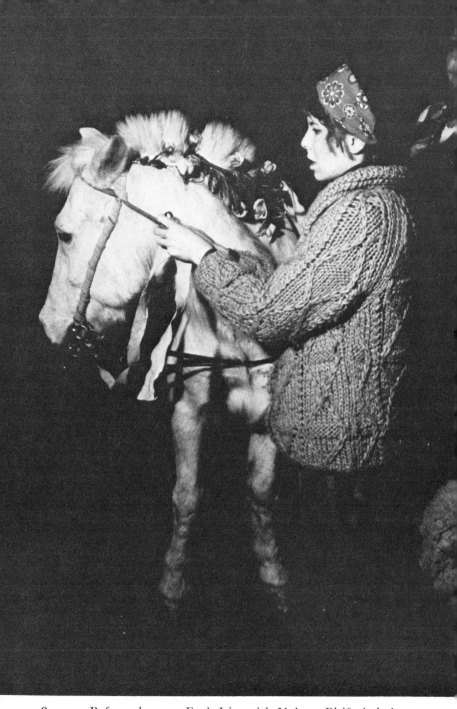

8   Before she met Earl, Liz, with Volney Phifer's help, gets Jordan ready for an appearance at the Metropolitan Opera.

Earl with a young cougar, 1968.

10   On the day Liz brought her home, Mignon sniffs out Jenny and Dog.

11   Mignon, now four months old.

12
Mignon entertains
at a birthday party.

Mignon at a benefit for Muscular Dystrophy.   **13**

Earl discovers one of Mignon's "tickle" spots.

Mignon tries on a new winter coat. **15**

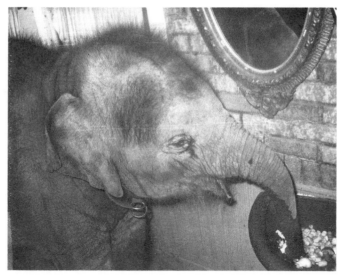

16   Mignon picks out her favorite vegetables from her bowl.

17   A partial family portrait: Mignon, Luther Owl, Liz, Buster Brown, Jenny, Robert Bobcat, and Dandelion.

Mignon and Dandelion enjoy a spring day.   **18**

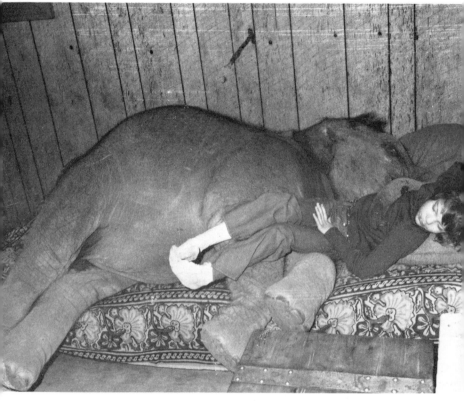

19   Jenny and Mignon nap together.

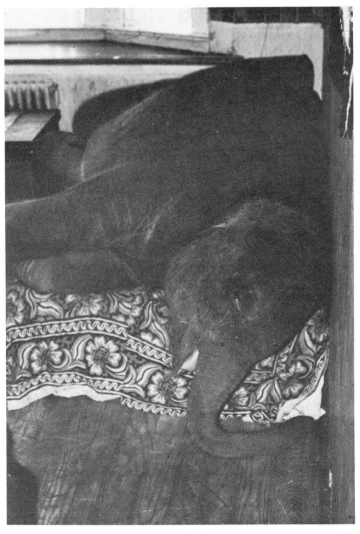

Mignon about to outgrow her bed. **20**

4

Mignon Earns Her Keep

Mignon's arrival gener-
ated a tremendous amount of publicity in the local
and national press. As word spread that a baby elephant was available for different functions, Mignon
began to earn her keep.

Mignon's first public appearance fulfilled one of
Liz's fantasies. When the Sells-Grey Circus was appearing in Port Richmond, Staten Island, the owners, who
were old friends of Volney's, stopped by for a visit.
At first sight of Mignon, they urged Liz and Earl to
bring her to the circus for a performance. It had only
been five days since Mignon's arrival in New Jersey,
and she could do no tricks, but the owners knew
that just the sight of such a tiny elephant would
charm their audiences.

All her life, Liz had wanted to be in a circus. That
night, Volney, Earl, Liz, Niki, Jenny, and Mignon
piled into the Volkswagen and drove to Port Richmond. As they pulled into the circus lot, Liz put her

hand over Mignon's trunk. The circus had three huge elephants, and mature elephants are very unpredictable in their reactions to a strange new baby. They can be very maternal or very aggressive. "If a car can tiptoe, that's what we did," reminisces Liz. "I tried to impress upon Mignon the idea that she shouldn't make a sound."

The circus tent was on a big athletic field with a running track around it. Liz and Earl hid at the goal line opposite from where the elephants were kept. The owners of the circus were apprehensive that the sight and scent of Mignon would set off a stampede.

Just before intermission, Earl took the mike and walked into the center ring. He began speaking in his low-key, country-boy style: "I grew up in Nebraska, and I married a city girl. I had been warned that city girls could be a little kinky, but nobody told me she'd be wanting to bring an elephant into the living room. Seriously, my wife and I are the first people in the Western world to try to raise an elephant in the house with us, and we'd like you to meet her. . . ."

The spotlight swung to the Volkswagen. Mignon was released, and Liz ran ahead of her, holding her baby bottle. "I just took off, and she came chugging after me with her trunk straight out making all sorts of noises that added up to 'Mommy, Mommy, please don't leave me, don't leave me.' When we got to the center of the ring, I stopped, and people were clapping and laughing. She drank her baby bottle, which was her only trick. It's still her most reliable crowd pleaser. I loved it."

Mignon's first paying jobs were simply brief appearances at children's birthday parties. It was the easiest money Liz and Earl made. Parents would pay $100 to $250 plus transportation costs just to have Mignon there. She was not strong enough to give rides, but she was quiet and gentle, and children were thrilled just to be near her. She would drink soda and eat birthday cake and ice cream. "She was marvelous around children. I think it comes from having our own two in the house. She related to Niki and Jenny like sisters, and she always seemed very happy at children's parties. She was often even more patient than she was at home."

Mignon was in some demand, too, as an attraction at Republican luncheons and banquets. Once she was hired to attend a $100-a-plate Republican dinner at a very luxurious catering house in New Jersey. The floors were carpeted in plush turquoise; the walls papered with cut velvet. Mignon greeted the guests; she stood in the receiving line in the lobby under a crystal chandelier, and they shook her trunk gently as they went by. Her presence seemed to delight everyone, and the Republican committeewoman who had hired Liz and Mignon was congratulated on her ingenuity.

Just before the banquet was to begin, the committeewoman asked Liz if she and Mignon would go to the third floor where a private cocktail party was taking place for the guests of honor. Liz agreed and led Mignon to the elevators. Liz's friend, Carol, accompanied her. "As the elevator door shut, Mignon peed and pooped. It was the first time she had been on an elevator, and she did not like it. We were totally unprepared. Somebody else had rung for the elevator on the second floor, and we were juggling this mess around. We had a huge pile of poop on a little Kleenex and nowhere to put it. It was very hard to keep up with her with the bucket because she wanted to get out of the elevator. We kept getting to floors, and we'd push another button because we did not want to get out until we had it cleaned up. People would get a quick glimpse of a peeing elephant and two laughing women trying to juggle a huge pile of shit. The door would shut, and we'd see a group of amazed and startled faces. Then we'd hit another floor and the same thing would happen all over again. We were in that elevator for ten minutes before we finally got it all together in a bag. After that I learned to be very careful about taking her in elevators."

Mignon was only three months old when she was asked to appear in an outdoor production of the opera *Aïda* in Washington Crossing State Park in New Jersey. Before the performance, Liz took Mignon to Manhattan to outfit her. "We went to an Indian shop in Greenwich Village and bought bells and gold chains. The owner adored her and helped me fashion a bracelet for each foot. The opera company had a beautiful purple headpiece, and by the time we were finished, Mignon looked elegant. It was a funny, hokey performance. I was dressed as a slave girl who just happened to be carrying a bottle. The audience loved it when she came on stage, and the stage manager decided to milk it for all it was worth. He kept whispering, 'Go around again.' Then the orchestra would play the 'Triumphal March' over and over, and we'd walk in another circle and do a bow. People were laughing and laughing. Earl didn't come to rehearsals, but he came to one of the performances, and I saw him rolling around backstage."

Shortly after the *Aïda* performance, Liz received a telephone call from a lawyer living in Manhattan. He explained that he had seen a recent article about Mignon in the *New York Times,* and he wanted to rent her for an hour or so. All that he required was that Mignon wear a bonnet and wave a flag saying "Welcome Home, Dear" in her trunk.

Liz asked the man to tell her precisely what the occasion was and where Mignon would have to stand.

"My wife just had a baby," the lawyer explained. "She's taken the baby to the Midwest to visit her parents. She's been after me for months to build a nursery, but I never got around to it until after the baby was born. It's finally finished, and I want to surprise her by having an elephant dressed up as a baby waiting in the new nursery when she gets back."

"I was a little dubious as to how pleased his wife might be to find an elephant in her apartment, but the man seemed serious. So I agreed."

On the day that the mother and baby were due to return, Liz, Earl, and Mignon drove into Manhattan. It was getting dark as they arrived. The lawyer lived on 100th Street and Amsterdam Avenue, and it was difficult to find a place to park. Finally, Earl found a place a few blocks away. When Mignon and Liz got out of the Volkswagen, they were immediately surrounded by a crowd who could not believe a baby elephant had just stepped out of a Volkswagen bus into their neighborhood.

As they walked to the apartment house, about

thirty children accompanied them, bombarding them with questions about Mignon. As they turned the corner into 100th Street, Earl spotted a tough-looking security guard standing before the apartment complex. Intuition warned him that this was not going to be as easy a job as it had sounded over the phone. New York City has strict rules about where "exotic" animals can and cannot be taken.

Earl used a corner pay phone to call the client, who was embarrassed to admit that he had not checked it out with the guard, and he was sure the guard would *not* let them in. Couldn't they sneak her in somehow?

"Sneak in an elephant?!" asked Earl.

"She was small, but not that small," Earl recalls. "We had already attracted a large following. Liz, Mignon, and the kids hid behind a scrawny tree in the middle of the block. They looked like something out of an "Our Gang" comedy. I watched to see if the guard would leave his post. Finally, he did go somewhere, and I signaled Liz, who came running around the corner. Mignon followed, her stubby legs going as fast as they could. When we got to the entrance, the client buzzed us in. As we entered, I noticed that the closed circuit television monitoring system was pointing straight at us. Quickly I held a jacket over the camera and Liz and Mignon snuck by.

"Inside we found a typical small New York City apartment. The nursery was perhaps eight feet square, at the most eight by ten. It was filled with a crib, a playpen, a diaper-changing table, a toy chest, and stuffed animals. There was no place for Mignon. We rearranged the furniture and crammed Mignon in. We got the baby bonnet on her, and Liz had Mignon practice her rather anemic flag wave. Everything was ready. The wife was supposed to arrive at any moment. Half an hour went by, and then an hour. Finally, the lawyer called the airline and discovered the plane was delayed. He begged us to stay, and Liz and I didn't have the heart to leave.

"It was clear that he was a born showman trapped into being a lawyer. He loved expansive gestures. This was his first child, and he was treating the birth like an extravaganza. He showed us a picture of what the apartment looked like on the day his wife came home from the hospital. He had bought her a dozen roses for every day she was pregnant. The apartment was filled with over 3,000 roses. Once Liz and I saw that photograph, it seemed perfectly natural that he should hire Mignon for his wife's homecoming, and she wanted to help him out.

"Mignon was wonderful. She stood in the nursery, surrounded by all those flimsy baby things and didn't knock over or step on a thing. Liz taught her to play the toy piano while we were waiting. Once she figured out that it was her trunk that made the music, she kept at it for over an hour. Later, I got her one of her very own.

"Finally, after two hours, the wife arrived. Her husband led her into the nursery. Mignon waved her flag and lifted one foot, showing off her entire prepared repertoire in one stroke. The new mother kept saying she was 'thrilled, really thrilled.' There wasn't much else she could say. After the surprise, we figured it was time to leave; the man was happy and thanked us profusely.

"On the way out, the security guard was back. We decided to march right past him. The worst he could do was to kick us out, and we were on our way out anyway. The guard's face almost dissolved when he saw an elephant coming out of an apartment—especially as he hadn't seen one go in. He reprimanded us, saying, 'Elephants are not allowed on the grounds.' I said we weren't on the grounds, just in an apartment.

"Out on the street, the kids were waiting for us. Their number had doubled, as several had made bets with their friends over whether there really *was* an elephant in the neighborhood. We talked to them for nearly an hour, answering questions, and giving the littlest ones rides. They had a ball."

All animal trainers who allow their animals to mingle with the public fear that somebody will be hurt. Liz and Earl know that no matter how much Mignon is provoked, if she ever hurts anyone the insurance company will never let her work in public again. But because she has a close and very warm relationship with humans, they feel that Mignon will never initiate an aggressive move. Their main worry is that someone will provoke her deliberately. They have tried to teach her not to react, no matter what the provocation; this, of course, is extremely difficult to teach an animal whose first instinct is to protect herself.

When she was very young, Mignon was too vulnerable-looking for anyone to treat her maliciously or even mischievously. However, as Mignon got bigger, Liz discovered that boys between the ages of nine and fourteen seemed to delight in trying to torment her. They pulled her tail and pinched her trunk. "I know that sounds sexist," says Liz, "but it was true. Little girls never gave me any trouble. They always acted sweet and even maternal around her, but boys seemed to want to test their bravery on her.

"At first Mignon never did a thing to fight back. Finally, a boy bothered her one time too many, and she turned around and gave him a swat with her trunk. It wasn't much of a swat. It shocked the boy more than it hurt him, but it sent shudders through me.

"I knew that Mignon had a perfect right to swat him. He shouldn't have been hitting her and poking her, but I couldn't let her do things like that, especially as she got bigger and stronger. I told her, 'NO!' and rapped her on the trunk. I knew she understood because she looked ashamed, but I still had to figure out a way to make sure it did not happen again. I began taking an extra person along on all jobs.

"When I'm alone, I cannot watch what someone might be doing to Mignon's tail or hind legs. Having someone stand behind Mignon helped to solve the problem. I also became adept at using the elephant hook, not just on Mignon, but on the public. If I saw a boy pinching her or poking her even after I had asked him to stop, I would watch him. As he reached for a part of Mignon's body, so would I, and I'd rap him hard with the elephant hook. Then I'd look at him in mock horror and say, 'Oh, I'm so sorry.' It worked every time. The tormentors would leave. They never knew if I did it on purpose or by accident, but they'd leave and that's all I cared about."

In truth, Mignon has always been much more patient about being abused by children than Liz. For example, one day she was appearing in Central Park at a benefit for retarded children. There were almost 4,000 people in Central Park's Sheep Meadow. One boy about twelve years old was autistic. He had never learned to talk; he could only express himself in occasional violent outbursts. As he stood near Mignon, he suddenly exploded into one of his violent cycles. Two nurses tried to contain him as he spastically jabbed his fingers at Mignon's eyes. Then he grabbed her trunk, squeezed, and twisted it with all his strength. Mignon bounced away a step, squeaking in obvious pain. The two nurses tugged on the boy, and Mignon freed her trunk. She stood and watched as the two adults tried desperately and ineffectually to subdue him. Then she took a step forward and wrapped her trunk around the boy's shoulders. She cradled him with her trunk and began to rock him slowly and rhythmically.

Liz reached out to pull Mignon away, afraid she was hurting the boy. Then she saw the expression on his face and stopped. The violent twitching was gone. In its place was a quiet smile. Mignon appeared to be throwing her entire weight into the rocking motion. She weighed about 300 pounds then, nearly four times the boy's weight. After about sixty seconds, Mignon unwrapped her trunk. The boy sank to the ground, playing quietly with her toes. Then he sat up cross-legged at Mignon's feet and watched her calmly and happily.

His nurses were amazed. They told Liz that rocking was a technique only recently discovered to have a calming effect on autistic children. They could not believe that Mignon had done it instinctively.

"Mignon just seemed to sense something was wrong," says Liz. "Right before she started to rock him, I saw her run her trunk up and down his body. I don't know what she felt, but something must have told her his rhythm was all off, and to straighten out his rhythm she had to rock him."

Some of Mignon's jobs were less successful. A rock group called Elephant's Memory hired her for their press party at the Fillmore East concert hall in New York. Their record had been produced by the Beatles' company, Apple Records, and John and Yoko Lennon had promised to come to the party.

When Liz, Earl, and Mignon arrived at the Fillmore, the press agent came out to meet them with buckets of red paint. He wanted to paint a big apple on Mignon's side. He swore it was body paint that would wash off easily. Liz reluctantly agreed.

It was very noisy and crowded in the main room, but according to Liz, Mignon seemed to enjoy herself. "It was acid rock, exactly the kind of music she would hate if I put it on my record player at home, but she is such a ham, she acted as if she loved it. I didn't really enjoy myself. Many of the people were weird, and I was worried one of them would think it was funny to try to get her high."

Finally, John and Yoko arrived. The press wanted to get pictures of them with the elephant, but people kept crowding around. "I noticed Yoko didn't want to get too close to Mignon, but I didn't pay too much attention. It was such a madhouse I just wanted the job to be over. Finally, the photographers pushed us all into the ladies' room—John, Yoko, Earl, Mignon, and me. Yoko moved all the way to the back. It was then I realized she was petrified of Mignon. The look on her face was sheer panic. Before the photographers could get set up, she grabbed Lennon and ran."

The next day, Liz tried to wash the apple off. There are two different versions of why it didn't come off. Liz's is simple: The press agent lied and used an oil-based paint that water could not wash off.

Earl says, "The only thing I can tell you about that apple is that Mignon wouldn't let Liz wash it off. Every time Liz brought the water hose out, Mignon would step on it. Mignon knew if she stepped on it, the water wouldn't come out. The water was cold, and she didn't like it. Mignon loves to play games. She'd let Liz wash her trunk, her face, and her ears, but every time Liz moved to Mignon's side or back Mignon would step on the hose. Then the elephant would turn around and split—just out of hose reach. Liz would be standing there yelling with frustration. It was something to see. Liz finally came in and dried off. She'd had *her* bath. The elephant never really got one. Eventually, the apple faded away to just a memory." ✎

Shortly after the fiasco at the Fillmore, Mignon was asked to participate in a skit with members of the sales department of the New York Telephone Company. Once a year, the company throws a banquet for all its executives, and different groups within the company compete with different skits. Each tries to outdo the others with elaborate costumes and props, and the sales department decided that a baby elephant would be a coup.

The banquet took place at the Biltmore Hotel in Manhattan. Mignon's job was simply to go up three or four carpeted stairs, follow the sales department personnel into the banquet hall, and then run around the hall once with them. Everything went fine except just as it was time for Mignon to go up the stairs, one of the executives decided to help her by giving her a push.

"He thought he was helping, but he pushed her right onto her trunk," recalls Liz. "The stairs were covered with a smooth carpet and kind of slick. Her feet went out from under her, and she slid halfway down to the floor. She couldn't figure out how to get up. Meanwhile, this executive was sprawled on top of her, determined to help. Finally, Earl got him off her as politely as possible, and shouldered her back up. She did fine once left to her own devices. Off we toddled; we ran full tilt to catch up with our group, with Mignon moving her fat legs as fast as she could to keep up. They were thrilled with the whole thing. As so often happens, the banquet started hours late, so we had to wait three or four hours. The management kept coming in and out to make sure she was all right, and they all fell in love with her.

"When they found out we also had a chimpanzee at home, they hired us to officiate at the opening of an elegant bar and restaurant in the center of the hotel lobby. Donna Rae passed around hors d'oeuvres. She is marvelous at the job, as long as it's one for her and one for the customer. Mignon just walked around sipping people's drinks and eating ice cubes.

"Taking Mignon to jobs like that was just like taking a toddler. Sometimes she got bored with having to stand still for long. There was a flight of eight or ten stairs in the restaurant, and she spent hours going up and down, just like a little kid. She learned to balance herself by using her trunk as a tripod as she was going down. She amused herself and entertained all the people at the bar in the process."

Perhaps Mignon's most unusual job came when she was about six months old. Liz received a call from a man who said he belonged to an amateur theater group in Washington, D.C., that was producing a political satire. They wanted the "first lady" of the show to ride an elephant onto the stage. Mignon at this time had given rides only to children, so Liz asked the weight of the actress. The man answered, "Oh, maybe a hundred and twenty-five pounds." Liz told him that was the maximum Mignon could carry, and that she could carry it for only a minute or two.

The man was quick to agree to this and to the fee Liz quoted. Rarely had a potential client made his mind up so quickly. The caller arranged to meet them outside the city because, he explained, it was a little difficult to find the theater.

Earl was not planning to go, and Liz had arranged for her friend Carol to join her. However, the weather turned bad, and Earl began to worry about Liz running into trouble on the road with the elephant, so he decided to come along as well.

They got to Washington without incident and went to the arranged meeting place. A car pulled up, and three men came to greet them dressed in tuxedos with red sashes. In the backseat of their car sat three women in satin. Each wore a fur stole and an elaborate beehive hairdo. Liz turned to Earl and said, "I had no idea it was going to be this fancy."

The men told Liz and Earl to follow, and they

drove through a labyrinth of back alleys to a deserted part of the city. They were led down an alley to a building that looked like an old warehouse with boarded-up windows. "After I saw the place," says Liz, "I was very glad Earl had decided to come. If it had been Carol and me, I think we would have just turned around and come home."

Liz stayed in the bus with Mignon as Earl got out to discuss logistics. The warehouse, it turned out, was the theater. Earl accepted that, but he needed to know exactly when and where they wanted Mignon. Meanwhile, one of the women got out of the backseat and came to chat with Liz. She was very tall and had a deep voice and stubby fingers. When Earl came back to the truck, Liz said, "Hey, uh, I'm not too sure about this whole thing. I think that *she* was a *he*."

"Don't be ridiculous," said Earl.

They unloaded Mignon and began to brush her for the performance. Suddenly, the back door of the theater opened, and the chorus line came out. They were dressed in spangled tank-top outfits of red, white, and blue. As they came closer, Liz and Earl saw that their legs, encased in black net stockings and high heels, were unusually sturdy. It was clear, suddenly, that all of them were men. Liz started to laugh. Earl just opened his mouth and stared.

Then the first lady arrived. Her name was Liz, she was about six feet two inches, and she weighed close to 200 pounds. She was wearing a white satin gown, black net stockings, high heels, and layers of makeup over his five o'clock shadow.

At that time, Mignon stood about four feet high at the shoulder. "Earl and I held a quick conference.

We decided that as long as we were there to help, it wouldn't hurt Mignon to carry the first lady for just a few seconds. Mignon had given Earl short rides and was much stronger than she looked.

"The first lady, on the other hand, was much more delicate than she looked. She kept exclaiming, 'Oh, I don't know if I can ever get up on that thing! She's so big. I'm afraid I'll fall off.' Earl had to help her mount but wasn't sure how to do it. He was tempted to hoist her up, but she was acting so ladylike that he hesitated because of her squirmishness. Finally, he ended up practically shoveling her up on top of Mignon. She sat there astraddle, arranged her gown, and we led them in for the 'inauguration.'

"It turned out that we had been hired by an association of gay people in Washington, most of them government workers with good jobs and lots of money to spend. What looked like an old warehouse was in reality a $250,000 converted theater. Next door was a nightclub discotheque."

In recalling the incident, Earl says, "They didn't invite us to their nightclub, which really disappointed me. The theater was gorgeous, so I can just imagine what the disco must have been like. They were charming people to deal with—the only thing that was staggering was the size of the first lady."

5

Earl's First Commercials

Mignon's jobs helped pay her enormous food bill, but supporting a household of two adults, two children, and an elephant is not a light responsibility, and both Liz and Earl worked full time. While Liz supervised most of Mignon's jobs, Earl continued to run the petting zoo at Coney Island. It was a two-hour commute from Volney's, and Earl often worked eighteen hours a day. "It was a summer of lousy weather, with particularly bad rainstorms on holidays. I couldn't afford to pay anyone to help me with the animals. We had a contract, but weeks went by and we were not paid. Finally, I told them I'd have to take the show someplace else in order to make some money.

"Shortly after that, I got a phone call in the middle of the night. The entire show had been stolen from the lot—all my animals. Luckily, the one animal I was closest to, Donna Rae, was home with me. I never left her out there. But I had goats, sheep, ponies, a miniature bull, and a large South American yellow-leg tortoise, about forty-five pounds. The tortoise was a wonderful animal. He liked to sit at my feet like a puppy, and when I got up he would follow me. My German shepherd, Baron, was found running along the beach, but all the other animals had completely disappeared. Now, I was used to things going a little screwy since I met Liz, but to have an entire animal show stolen seemed to be the last straw."

The robbery brought Earl publicity, but not the kind he would have chosen. He did a tape for the local TV stations, pleading for the return of his animals. Aside from the substantial monetary loss that the theft represented, he was worried that the animals might die if they were not cared for.

The next night a woman in Brooklyn called the police. She had heard strange noises coming from an abandoned tin shed. The police investigated and found the shed full of animals, all suffering from heat and dehydration. The shed had no windows, and the animals had been left to die without food or water. Earl was able to save most of them, although a few were never found, including the South American tortoise. The mystery of who stole the animals and why was never solved.

"After I got my animals back, I decided to cut the Coney Island job as a dead loss. Mignon's career was picking up, and Liz often needed me to help her. Mignon brought in some money, but I was sick of just surviving. All my life I had dreamed of owning my own land, of having the freedom to work with animals in my own way. I was in my thirties, and I was discouraged. All my dreams about working with birds of prey or endangered species seemed impossible.

"Volney was a generous man, but extremely possessive and very set in his ways. The place needed so much work, and yet I felt I couldn't pick up a hammer because Volney would resent it if I made repairs. The robbery of the petting zoo was like a depressing joke. It almost wiped me out, but it made me realize I didn't want to spend the rest of my life living at Volney's and taking barnyard animals around to shopping malls and amusement parks."

Shortly after the robbery, Earl received a phone call from Dancer, Fitzgerald, and Sample, an advertising agency that had heard he had a well-trained chimp. The agency needed a chimp for a commercial for B.P. Filling Stations. The firm was inaugurating a campaign to give away a free Bic "Banana" pen with every purchase. The chimp was to drive a cut-down Model T Ford into a gas station, turn off the motor, buy gas, and point to the windshield, indicating that it was to be cleaned. Then the chimp was to scrawl an X for a signature on the charge and drive off, pen in hand. The executive said they were interviewing a number of trainers and asked Earl to bring in Donna Rae for an audition.

Earl and Donna Rae drove into the city to the agency's office on Madison Avenue. Donna Rae held Earl's hand as they stood in front of the receptionist waiting their turn. Once they were ushered into the executive's office, Donna Rae conducted the interview herself. She walked around to the executive and sat in his lap. She looked at the calendar and pictures on his desk, picked up the phone, and handed it to Earl. Many chimps are nervous and move jerkily. Donna Rae seemed perfectly relaxed. The agency was charmed both by her and Earl's relationship with her.

"Earl and Donna Rae seemed so at ease with each other," recalls the executive who hired them. "It was clear from the way they communicated with each other that Donna Rae would be willing to try anything Earl suggested. We saw several chimps and their trainers, but none had the rapport of Earl and Donna."

The commercial was to be Earl's introduction to the "hurry-up-and-wait" syndrome of most television production. The commercial was needed right away. The agency wanted to know how soon Donna Rae could be trained. Earl told them he would need a week. The hardest part would be to train Donna Rae to drive the little fiberglass Model T. The executive then asked Earl to get started right away.

"Fine," replied Earl. "When can I get the car you want Donna Rae to drive?"

There was an awkward pause: It seemed the car was not quite ready. It finally arrived just two days before the commercial was to be shot.

The car, built to one-quarter scale, was about five-and-a-half feet long. Earl put the car in the driveway and showed it to Donna Rae. Naturally curious, Donna Rae opened the door and squirmed into the driver's seat. It seemed she understood exactly what was expected of her. Earl turned on the ignition. The engine of the little Model T, which was located right under the driver's seat, had a roar like a diesel truck. It sounded as though the car was exploding under her, and Donna Rae leaped into Earl's arms, chattering with fear. Earl tried to coax her back into the driver's seat, but she refused.

"I knew I shouldn't force her. She wasn't being difficult; she was just frightened. I turned the engine off and went inside for four or five different kinds of soda pop. Donna Rae loves pop, especially orange, Coke, Seven-Up, and root beer. I think it took about a six-pack of pop to get her back in the car. She knew that every time she sat there, I'd give her a sip. Then we practiced turning the engine on. I knew she would get used to it eventually. It was not as if she was inherently afraid of motors; she and I had probably driven 10,000 miles together. And by the end of the day she was having a wonderful time driving around our driveway.

"We spent some time practicing with the pen, but I wasn't worried about that part. When we traveled together with the petting zoo, I often gave Donna Rae a pen and pad to keep her amused. To rehearse her for the commercial, I played the part of the gas station attendant. I'd hand her the pen and her bill, and she learned to scribble something on the bill and hand it back to me."

On the day of the shooting, Earl arrived early to accustom Donna Rae to the new setting. He introduced her to the actor who would be playing the attendant and to the cameramen on the crew. Suddenly another trainer arrived with a chimp in his arms.

"It could have been an explosive situation," says

Earl. "If there is one rule of etiquette among animal trainers, it is that you do not bring a strange animal onto a set because it can easily cause a distraction, or worse, a fight. However, this gentleman had heard about the commercial, and knowing I was relatively inexperienced in the making of TV commercials, he had decided to bring his own chimp. When I confronted him, he said he had only come to watch, but I knew he was there in the hope that I would foul up and his chimp would get the job.

"I was furious, but I was still new to the business. I didn't want to make waves by insisting the man and his chimp be thrown off the set. It was left to Donna Rae to handle the situation and she did. She could sense that she was the star, and she completely ignored the other chimp.

"Donna drove the car down into the filling station and stopped exactly where she was supposed to. At least on the screen that's what you see. She stopped because she knew I was hidden behind the pump with a can of soda pop.

"Then we tried to film the close-up of the attendant handing the pen to Donna Rae. She does have a small thumb, but it is set at a different angle from ours and the pen had to be pointed down for her to grab it. The actor kept handing the pen to her with the tip pointing at her. She kept fumbling and dropping it. It got her terribly upset. I showed the actor exactly how to hand it to her, but he couldn't get it right. There are some actors who, though they may be perfectly competent in other situations, freeze when they have to work with an animal. Some aptitude with animals should be part of the casting requirements for commercials with animals, but it seldom is.

"It was my first important television job, and I had begun to understand its frustrations. Your animal is working and doing exactly what is in the script. Then the lighting is wrong or a camera isn't working, and you have to get the animal to do it again and again. The animal becomes confused or else it gets bored or tired and wants to rest when everybody else is ready."

Donna Rae had to do about half a dozen takes, and still it wasn't quite right. On the seventh take, as she drove into the filling station, a tire exploded. Donna Rae jumped out of the car with a look of panic on her face and fled into Earl's arms.

The mechanics repaired the tire, and Earl coaxed Donna back for another take. The actor finally thrust the pen at Donna so she could hold onto it. Donna Rae added her own little fillip to the commercial by drawing a perfect X on the bill.

"I really don't believe the perfect X was pure chance. Donna Rae was having a ball. She loved the attention, and she enjoyed having a complicated task to perform. She remembered everything that was expected of her, including pointing to the windshield in order to have it cleaned. I really do believe that an intelligent animal like Donna senses the excitement and pressure of making a movie or television commercial. At the moment of stress, they go beyond what they have practiced and sometimes give a little more.

"The experience was tremendously satisfying for me. For all its difficulties, Donna and I surmounted most of them. The client was tremendously pleased, but more than that, it was richly satisfying to use Donna to her fullest potential."

Earl's next job was for the Hartford Insurance Company. Their advertising agency came up with the idea of bringing the Hartford stag symbol to life. They envisioned a series of commercials featuring a live stag who was to be shown peering into houses, autos, and store windows in order to dramatize the need for different types of insurance coverage.

However, every trainer they approached said it was impossible. Naturally, the agency wanted a stag with a full rack of antlers, but unfortunately at that time the stag is going through hormonal changes that make him very aggressive. It was a conundrum. Because of the hormones, the stag was a magnificent symbol of strength with its full rack and swelling neck muscles. But because of the hormones, the stag at its peak of physical beauty also had the instinct to fight all other males and was extremely irritable. All the trainers told the agency it would be impossible to work with a stag in full rut. Full rut is the breeding season of deer. For deer, unlike cattle, goats, and sheep who retain their horns for a lifetime, shed their antlers each year and grow new ones. The size of the antlers depends on the state of maturity of the animal and the amount, quality, and mineral content of their feed.

The agency called Earl as a last resort. Earl showed Volney the script and asked his opinion, and Volney agreed with the other trainers. Even when they are not in rut, stags are extremely difficult and nervous animals to train. "If it could be done at all," said

Volney, "and I doubt if it can, it will take you six months to a year." The agency needed to begin shooting the commercial in six weeks.

Earl decided to try it. "I have a different method of working with an animal than anybody else. I was stubborn enough to think I could do it even though everybody else said it couldn't be done . . . *if* I could find the right animal."

Earl's method is not outwardly different from that of other trainers. On the set he uses the usual reward system—a treat for every stunt performed. Earl's special method is based on the chemistry between himself and the animal. It requires finding an animal that he responds to and that will respond to him. "The selection of the proper animal is the reason for my success."

After telling the agency he would try to do the commercials, he was given money to find a stag. First, Earl called Ron Degonia, a rodeo clown from Missouri, whom he had met through his network of contacts. Ron was used to working around rough stock and would be aware of the dangers. Earl felt he would be helpful in his search for a stag. Together they traveled up and down the Eastern seaboard, looking for the right animal.

Using his and Volney's network of contacts, Earl called several animal preserves asking if they had a suitable animal. At a Pennsylvania game farm they found a very gentle stag. Earl knew after fifteen minutes that he'd be able to work with this deer and establish the kind of quick rapport that was needed. However, the stag's antlers were not symmetrical, and he was undersized in the haunches. Reluctantly, Ron and Earl decided to look further.

In a shooting preserve in Tennessee, where hunters pay to shoot animals in a confined acreage, Earl and Ron found their deer. He had a beautiful rack and bearing. He moved with authority, and Earl knew he would photograph well. Unfortunately, Earl could tell that the deer had a difficult personality. "He was not flighty or unworkable," says Earl. "He was just tough and arrogant."

Ask Earl how he can tell the personality of a deer and he looks up incredulously. "Don't you get first impressions of people? It's the same with an animal. Every one of them is an individual. Forget that and you do not belong in this business. If you know what to look for, an animal will let you know it is the one for you. However, it is also true that a lot of animals have proven rather quickly that I'm a liar."

Earl bought the deer from the shooting preserve and named him Moose. "I know he would have been killed if he had stayed there. He was a magnificent trophy for a hunter. He is much too beautiful an animal to be shot by a hunter in a preserve when he could be shot by camera and millions could enjoy him on the screen."

When they returned to Volney's, Earl set up a large pen and began to work. The first step was to take Moose off his regular two-meals-a-day schedule. Moose was only fed if he ate out of Earl's hand or if he walked to where Earl wanted him to go. "The thing that made it so difficult for Moose was the fact that he really isn't gentle. I had to turn him around and gain his confidence and respect. I didn't want to put a halter on him and lead him. In the first place, it would have taken me months to try to halter-train him. In the second place, it would change his spirit to halter-train him. I didn't want to do it. I knew the commercials would be a great success if I could keep Moose's arrogance intact." After a few days, Moose would accept food from Earl's and Ron's hand.

The advertising agency executives came out to watch Earl in action. They were impressed with Moose's beauty, but less impressed with Earl's technique. They'd peer through the chain-link fence and see Earl sitting on his haunches talking to the deer. Sometimes Moose would come and eat an apple out of his hand; more often, Moose would just ignore him. It certainly did not look as if Moose considered Earl important at all, much less that Earl would be able to lead Moose through the complicated script they had prepared. For example, Moose was to walk up a flight of stairs onto a porch, look into a window, and push a tricycle. If Earl could not get Moose to eat an apple on command, how could the advertising agency believe Earl would ever get him to do everything they had in mind in only four weeks?

As the days went on, the executives worried more and more. They had convinced the Hartford Insurance Company that the commercials would be a success, and now they themselves were not confident. They urged Earl to stop fooling around and get on with the training.

"I just don't work in a traditional manner. Even Liz used to get upset with me because she thought I was just fooling around. I don't crack the whip. I don't repeat and repeat. It takes tremendous effort and concentration to win the animal's trust, but once I've done that, I figure the animal and I can do whatever it is we're asked to do. But first, I have to get in tune with the animal, and while I'm doing that there's not much to see. It would have been foolish to try and subdue Moose. If he panicked, I'd have run the risk of breaking his neck or an antler."

Meanwhile, Earl could see progress, even if no one else could. Moose had learned to go to different points of the pen looking for food. One of the commercials called for Moose to nudge a tricycle on a sidewalk because the creator of the commercial thought it would be visually interesting to see a stag's head next to a tricycle. Earl took apart a tricycle seat and built a new one with a tiny storage space under the top. He put corn inside the seat, and Moose learned to flip the tricycle seat up in order to get his food. The spring had to be quite delicate so that Moose would not topple the tricycle over out of frustration.

After only four weeks of training, Earl drove Moose to California for the shooting. The director was an extremely patient man. If Moose started to go to a certain point on the set and then stopped, he would film what he could and told Earl not to worry; they would be able to splice the pieces together. "He had the patience of Job," says Earl. "It was my first job on that scale, and I was nervous. The agency was twice as nervous as I was. The filmmaker was an island of calm. We couldn't have done it without him."

On the day they were to shoot Moose and the tricycle, the agency had arranged for a phony elk's head to be brought to the set. They didn't believe Moose could do it, and they were prepared to have a stage-hand push the tricycle across the sidewalk.

Earl brought his trick tricycle onto the set. However, on this day he wired the seat shut. He told the director to get ready to film and then he let Moose out of the trailer. Moose walked up the sidewalk toward the tricycle. Then, as if he were reading the script, he bent down and nudged at the tricycle seat, expecting the top to flip open. When it didn't, he nudged it again, applying more pressure, and the tricycle slowly moved across the sidewalk onto the grass. "That sounds great, doesn't it, but it didn't happen that way," Earl adds. "Everyone waited about thirty-five minutes for Moose to relax after being brought onto the set. Moose made three or four practice runs and then he was ready. It seems Moose wanted us to appreciate him. We did."

Everyone on the set spontaneously burst into applause. "It was a wonderful moment," recalls Earl. "I am as proud of that one moment as of anything else in my professional career, because Moose and I had worked so hard to achieve it. Everyone in the animal business understood what a tremendous accomplishment those commercials were. It is much more dramatic to work with a lion or a bear, but the animal people all appreciate the stag commercials. Remember Moose never once had a halter or a lead line on him. All of the commercials were shot in an enclosed set, and Moose was loose. At any moment he could have panicked and destroyed the set or destroyed himself, but he remained calm the entire time, and he is not a calm animal. His personality never changed, but he had learned to accept my presence and the ten to thirty others on the set. He did things no one would expect a stag to do in the short time spent. What a super animal!"

6

Flood and Death at Volney's

Even though the Hartford commercials brought in a substantial amount of money, the bulk of it went to balance out accounts. Animals do not get residuals for commercials, so Moose's payment was in one lump sum.

Earl felt no closer to any of his dreams. He still did not have nearly enough capital to buy his own land. Furthermore, although the work with Moose had been challenging, Moose himself did not have the intelligence to provide a totally satisfying relationship such as the one between Liz and Mignon.

"I came back from California feeling vaguely dissatisfied," says Earl. "I felt that Liz and I had to work too hard just to survive. We never seemed to get anywhere. It was like treading water. Then, a few days after I got back, we were literally underwater and I didn't have time to think about anything but survival."

Volney's farm is located in the hollow of what is

already a flood plain in New Jersey. Volney was used to floods. He kept a rowboat tied to the back of the house.

Coming from the plains of Nebraska, Earl was appalled at the periodic inundation of the farm. It had happened several times since Earl had moved there. The water overflowed the banks of Volney's lily ponds and crept up the pathways toward the animal cages. It never got so high as to threaten the animals, but it frightened Earl. "I had never been around high water. If there's a fire, you can always grab water or a fire extinguisher or call the fire department. There's a chance of putting it out. But in a flood you're helpless. The water keeps coming and coming, and there's not a thing you can do about it."

Earl returned with Moose early in November. At the same time that he was arriving from the northwest, gale force winds and driving rains had been coming in from the southeast. New Jersey was being hit by the backlash of a tropical storm from the Caribbean.

The wailing of the winds and the turbulence of the storm terrified Mignon. She spun around in circles, making high-pitched, squeaking noises. She threw herself at Liz, nuzzling her head under Liz's armpit. Jenny and Niki tried to convince her there was nothing to worry about. Both Jenny and Niki were excited by the storm. They had lived through floods before and knew that no matter how bad the rain got, it would not get to the house.

But while Niki and Jenny thought the storm was fun, Liz was concerned. She had never seen rain come down like this. The wind was whipping the raindrops together into great torrential sheets. When Liz and Earl went out to check on the animals, they discovered that the rain was coming down so fast it was hard to breathe. It was like walking through something solid.

Earl told Volney they had better move the animals to high ground. Volney said not to worry; it was just a thunderstorm.

Earl argued that even if it proved unnecessary, they would be better off moving the animals while there was still light. Volney was offended. He had run the farm for thirty years by himself, and he was not used to sharing authority. Earl and Volney shouted at each other over the roar of the storm.

Finally, Earl slammed out of the house, shouting that he would move his own animals and Volney's animals could fend for themselves if he didn't care. The Tebinkas, Volney's closest neighbors, lived on high ground. They gave Earl permission to use their backyard. Earl put Moose in a trailer and drove him to the Tebinkas', where he would be safe. Then he put together portable cages for his other animals and moved them all into the neighbor's backyard.

Just before dusk, Volney admitted that perhaps it was time to move the animals to high ground. "Volney was old then and very set in his ways," says Earl. "I think he was frightened also. He knew it would be very difficult to try to move all the animals, and he didn't want to admit to himself that it would have to be done."

It was not yet five o'clock, but it might as well have been midnight; the storm had turned the sky black. Behind the house by the pond, the water was practically over Earl's head. He and Volney rowed across the overflowing pond. As they made their way to the cages, Volney slipped in the mud. Earl helped him to his feet, but as Volney started to walk, his leg buckled under him. He had torn a ligament in his right leg. Earl grasped Volney around the waist, half-carried him back to the rowboat, and rowed back to the house. Meanwhile, as the wind howled and tree limbs snapped, Mignon grew more and more terrified. Earl helped Volney up the stairs and into the house.

Liz poured Volney a tumbler of Old Grand-Dad. She asked Niki and Jenny if they would feel safe if she went outside to help Earl. "They were wonderful," recalls Liz. "They made coffee and soup for Volney and comforted Mignon. Thank God for them. Because they were used to responsibility they really knew how to act and keep their heads in an emergency."

When Liz went out with Earl, the water was almost three feet high on the paths of the cages. It had begun to flood the bottom of some cages and the animals were terrified. Liz and Earl knew they would have to move them all, yet almost none of the animals were tame.

"Under normal circumstances, you could never touch most of Volney's animals. He had badgers, several fox, baboons, monkeys, and African porcupines who had almost never been handled. Earl and I were extremely worried that they would give us a hard time, but it was extraordinary. They seemed to understand that we were their only hope of survival. We each took a rowboat and went out to their cages. When we opened their doors, they would jump in. Animals who are natural-born enemies sat peacefully in the same rowboat—badgers and foxes and chickens, for example. On one trip, I filled the boat with almost two dozen rabbits. They were all shivering, but they sat on the seats, lined up in perfect rows, and I felt as if I were living out a scene from *The Wind in the Willows.*"

By the time they had gotten all the smaller animals to safety at the Tebinkas', it was well into the night and still raining. Earl slogged his way to the far pastures, which were on slightly higher ground. Yet even there, the near end of the deer pen was underwater. The deer were crowded into the far corner, obviously petrified. Even if they did not drown, Earl realized they would die of fright if he did not get them out.

The Tebinkas helped Earl build a corral in their backyard out of portable panels from the petting zoo and Earl's Arctic show. Earl and Liz went back into the water to try to bring the deer out. "I have never been so cold and wet in my life," says Liz. "I was completly numb and frightened that they would all die. I didn't know how we were going to move the deer. Not one of those deer had ever had a halter on.

"Earl and I half swam and half waded in the cold, murky water toward the deer. Earl slung a rope around a deer's neck. The water was so high that both Earl and the deer had to swim, but the animal swam right alongside Earl. I watched Earl do it once, then put a rope around another deer. We had to be careful because their hooves are so sharp that they could have cut us badly.

"But they were unbelievably attentive to every move we made. For just a short distance, the water was over my head. Then it was around my hips, high enough so that the deer still had to swim, and they could swim faster than I could walk through the water. I'd give them a tug telling them to slow down, and they would.

"However, once we got onto high ground where they were safe, there was another thirty yards to the entrance of the corral, and they wanted to run away. With their feet on solid ground, they felt secure and wanted to escape. The hardest part was getting each of them into the corral, but we did it. Afterward, I couldn't believe it. Volney had over 150 animals, and we had moved them all without losing one. I felt as if we had pulled off a miracle."

It was seven o'clock in the morning when Liz and Earl returned to the house, but the day had no dawn. It was raining as hard as before, and there was almost no light. Inside they found Jenny and Niki asleep on the floor. Mignon lay on her bed, her trunk dangling over Jenny's head. Volney said he had told Niki and Jenny to go to sleep in their own beds, but they hadn't wanted to leave Mignon. Volney's leg was throbbing, and Liz suggested calling a doctor, but Volney did not trust doctors and he told her to stop fussing, that he would be fine.

Niki and Jenny woke up and wanted to know if the animals were safe. They wanted to go out right away to look at them, but Liz and Earl told them to go back to sleep. A few hours later, when the sky had turned from black to dark gray, Liz, Earl, and the children went to the Tebinkas' to check on the animals.

One deer stood in the corner of the pen with blood caked on his face. The entire left side of his antlers had been ripped off, leaving a hole that bored down into his skull. He was a young white-tailed buck about a year and a half old. As Earl walked toward him, the other deer scattered, but the wounded buck stood there trembling. Earl examined the wound. He found the broken antler lying on the ground near the fence and figured the buck must have charged into the fence in panic. The hole was inches deep; it appeared to go all the way down to the brain cavity.

"It's hopeless," said Earl, turning to Liz. "Go back and get my gun. I have to put him down."

Liz refused. "I was exhausted to the point of hysteria, and I didn't want to see that deer die. He had always been my favorite. Something in his bearing reminded me of Bambi's father. I insisted that we try to save him. I helped Earl carry the buck back to our house. He was paralyzed on his left side. Earl was too exhausted himself to argue with me."

Earl put the deer in the narrow back hallway, and Liz wedged him in with old blankets and pillows. Earl got out the peroxide and cleaned the wound. The deer was alert; he seemed to be soothed by the soft bedding surrounding him, for he did not struggle or thrash about.

Liz made soup for everybody and called Dr. Dorney. He arrived, took one look at the deer, and said, "He won't pull through. He isn't in any pain, but let me put him down."

Once again, Liz refused. "If he's going to die anyway and he's not in pain, it won't hurt to try penicillin." Reluctantly, after telling her she was a foolish romantic, Dorney gave Liz penicillin to be applied directly to the wound. Then he left, telling Earl the deer would be dead within twenty-four hours.

Liz applied the ointment to Bucky's wound. The next morning, he was still alive but not noticeably better. Liz tried to feed him, but all he seemed to want was water. The next day she fed him bananas and cookies. "I didn't care what he ate, as long as he would swallow it. I wanted to build up his strength. I'd bring him oatmeal and chocolate chip cookies and mash them into little crumbs. If I saw his nose twitch, I'd figure he liked it and that was what he got. Gradually, he gained strength, and the wound in his skull stopped oozing. He could stand, but his left side was still paralyzed. He couldn't walk."

The house had turned into a minihospital. Volney's leg had become painfully infected and kept him in bed for five weeks. On top of the infection, Volney was stricken with malaria, which afflicted him periodically. He had first caught malaria in the jungles of Indonesia in the 1920s. Liz and Earl took over all of Volney's chores.

While Volney recuperated, Bucky remained in the back hall. On some days he was able to stand and stagger around. On other days he could not move at all, and he would start to have convulsions.

One afternoon, about three weeks after the flood, Liz came home from grocery shopping to discover Bucky walking around the living room. Mignon sniffed at him curiously. Bucky seemed proud of his new sense of balance. His left side was stiff, but he carried himself erectly. Liz was gloriously happy. She decided to give him one more day in the house and then take him back to the pasture.

Bucky lived for over a year. He had become extremely tame, and as soon as he saw Liz, Niki, or Jenny he would run to the fence and eat an apple from their hands. One day, Liz noticed he was losing weight. She suspected worms and checked his stool and then wormed him, but he still continued to lose weight. One day, nearly a week later, she went out to the pasture and found him dead. She asked Dr. Dorney to perform an autopsy on him because she wanted to know what had happened. When Dorney performed the autopsy, he could not believe his eyes. Bucky's pelvis had been shattered and was bound together by sheaths of muscles. Dorney guessed that Bucky had smashed his pelvis the night of the flood and that during the months in the back hall, the muscles had filled in around his pelvis and held him together. He never limped or gave any indication he was in pain. It was a secondary infection that killed him.

Liz was saddened by Bucky's death. "Because I work around animals, naturally I have had to live with death as a fact of life, but I find it hard to accept a death of an animal I have cared for," she said.

At the public entrance to Volney's roadside zoo there is a sign that warns visitors: Do not expect a prettified view of nature. Birth and death and decay are natural. The laws of survival apply in a zoo as well as in the wild. My zoo is not for the squeamish.

Aside from the arrival of Mignon, the most exciting event of 1972 at Volney's zoo was the birth of two cubs to the old lioness Moira. No one even knew she was pregnant. Moira was nearly eighteen years old and thought to be well past the reproducing age. Earl, Liz, and Volney had noticed she was gaining weight, but they attributed it to the enriched food she was getting from Earl while Volney was recuperating. Then, one day when Earl went to feed her, he saw two tiny cubs, each only ten inches long. He ran into the house and summoned Volney and Liz. Volney's leg had not yet healed completely, and he hobbled out to the cage, using the new cane Liz had bought him.

He was delighted with the birth. As the three of them stood and watched the cubs tumble all over their mother, Liz became concerned. She noticed that the cubs were crying even with Moira's teats in their mouths. She told Earl and Volney she thought Moira had no milk because of her age. A few hours later, the cubs appeared to be getting weaker. Liz told Volney she thought she should bring the cubs into the house and bottle-feed them. Volney got angry.

"He accused me of trying to mother everything in sight," says Liz. "He felt they should stay with their natural mother. I could see they were not getting any milk. Finally, I told Volney that he had to let me in there or the cubs would die. Earl and I removed the cubs from the cage. Ordinarily, it would be extremely dangerous to try to take cubs away from their mother, but Moira was too befuddled to mind. I think her maternal instincts had been dulled with age. She just didn't know what to do with them."

Liz carried the cubs into the house in a blanket. She warmed up a baby bottle of milk, and the two cubs drank eagerly. After an hour or so, they were both visibly stronger. Later that night, Liz brought them into bed with her so she would hear them if they woke up hungry. Earl just rolled over on his side and went to sleep. "I figured that since I'd already shared my bed with an elephant, what difference could two lion cubs make?"

Niki and Jenny fell in love with the cubs, cuddling them, kissing them, and playing with them at every free moment. But Mignon was beside herself with jealousy. She watched Liz play with the cubs, heard Liz talking softly to them and giving them baby bottles, and then she went off to the corner to sulk. Within about ten days, the cubs were strong enough to start exploring. They showed no fear of Mignon, but Mignon wanted nothing to do with them.

"She went into a real sulk," says Liz. "She wanted nothing to do with anybody. She didn't want to do any of the usual lovey-dovey things we did together. I tried to reassure her, but she didn't respond."

However, after about three weeks or so, Liz noticed a change. One of the cubs, named Dandelion, was spending more and more of his time around Mignon's feet. Dandelion would try to climb Mignon's legs. Liz knew from experience that those tiny claws could be painful, but Mignon did not seem to mind. She wouldn't even try to shake Dandelion off. Instead, she wrapped her trunk around the cub and helped him climb. When he played at her feet, she'd tickle him in the stomach with hot air from her trunk.

Soon Dandelion deserted Liz and Earl's bed and started sleeping with Mignon. Mignon always made a place for him, shifting her body very carefully in order not to crush him.

Now it was Liz's turn to feel jealous. "It was the first time Mignon had shown that kind of love to anything except me. I was thinking of suing Dandelion for alienation of affection. She loved that cub. They became inseparable. He could do anything. He would run around under her legs full tilt, and she'd stop on a dime so as not to step on him."

When the lions got bigger, Liz put them outside in a big pen because they were too big to run around the house without being watched. The first night that Dandelion slept outside, Mignon wandered around the house looking for him. She walked over to Liz and nudged her with her trunk. "I know she was asking me where I had taken him and why. I explained it to her, but I don't think she thought it was fair. She was really annoyed with me."

The next morning, when Liz took Mignon out for her walk, Dandelion gave three high-pitched squeaks when he saw her, and Mignon made a beeline for his cage. Liz let Dandelion out, and the two animals began to play.

"After I let him out, Mignon would stand there and purr to him, feeling him all over with her trunk. Dandelion would jump all over her. Every day the two of them would act as if they hadn't seen each other for months.

"Then we'd all go for a walk. I felt like I was living in a fairy tale. We'd walk to a little hill beyond the pastures. There was a big oak tree on the top, and I'd sit in the shade with my back propped up against the trunk with Mignon, Dandelion, Niki, and Jenny playing in front of me, and I was the happiest person in the world."

"Once Dandelion and I were playing," recalls Niki of one of those idyllic days. "I guess Jenny and I started to get too rough, and Dandelion came over and knocked me down. I was so mad I took my finger and poked him hard on the back. He just ran shrieking over to Mignon. He was like a little crybaby running to Mommy and tattling. Mignon wrapped her trunk around him and comforted him like he was her child."

For four months, Dandelion remained Mignon's closest friend. Their daily walks together became routine. Then one morning, Liz went outside and discovered that Dandelion was very, very congested and could hardly breathe. Earl rushed him to Dr. Dorney, who sensed the problem was much too involved for the facilities of a dog and cat hospital. He suggested that the only hope of saving the cub was to take him to Cornell Veterinary College, which includes a center for the study of illness in exotic animals.

Earl wrapped Dandelion in a blanket and drove all night. They operated and put him in a respirator. They told Earl it made no sense for him to stay. They doubted that Dandelion would live. When they operated, the doctors were shocked to find that almost every organ in the cub's body was in the wrong place. The kidneys were distorted and malfunctioning, and the heart had been pushed aside by the stomach. Dandelion was a genetic freak, and it was a miracle that he had lived for six months. By the time Earl arrived back in New Jersey, the doctors had called to say that Dandelion was dead.

Liz cried. "I couldn't help thinking of the little

autistic boy that Mignon had comforted. I honestly believe that Mignon sensed from the beginning that Dandelion did not have long to live, and that is why she picked Dandelion out for a special friend.

"When Dandelion died, Mignon seemed to understand without being told. She didn't search for him. She just stood quietly, not really interested in anything. I knew that I didn't have to tell her Dandelion was dead. When we went outside the next day, she didn't even try to go over to his cage to look for him. She knew he was gone."

7

Enter Sasha

In the fall of 1972, while he was in the process of repairing the flood's damages, Earl received a phone call from Rod MacNicholl of the advertising agency Dancer, Fitzgerald, and Sample. MacNicholl asked Earl if he would come to his office to discuss a new campaign.

Hamm's Beer, sold throughout the Midwest, the South, and the Far West, had become a Dancer, Fitzgerald and Sample client. Rod MacNicholl had been assigned the task of creating a new image for Hamm's. Rod was eventually to become Earl's closest friend in the advertising business. "He doesn't belong on Madison Avenue," says Earl, paying Rod the ultimate compliment. "He belongs in the wilderness somewhere." Rod, who is an avid camper, does, in fact, spend nearly every free moment in the wilderness. He is also a long-distance runner and runs the fifteen miles from his home in Queens to Manhattan several times a week. He is a skilled storyteller who has perfected his tales of punishment on the marathon racing circuit to the same polished glint as Volney's tales of circus life. His impish, dry sense of humor connects nicely with Earl's country-boy funning.

For all the dour quality of Rod's favorite stories, his years on Madison Avenue have not made him cynical, though he would probably disagree. He works hard to make his commercials entertaining. "Just because we're trying to sell something, I don't see any reason to irritate people. If you make something beautiful or unusual or funny enough, people will remember the product."

When he called Earl, Rod had been working on a sixty-second fantasy about a man and a bear for Hamm's Beer. His storyboards showed a rugged, bearded man wandering through the wilderness with a large bear at his side. At the end, he pauses briefly and drinks Hamm's Beer. The concept was simple, but Rod believed that it would touch on many people's fantasies.

"I thought a lot of people would fantasize about what it would be like just hanging around with a bear, drinking beer, living in the beautiful woods. I know I'd rather be out there with the danger than going to the office on Madison Avenue every day grinding out commercials. And a lot of people want that, but they know they can't have it. So the next best thing is to look at it. We all have jobs to do and there's someplace else we'd like to be. That's what these ads are about, using a rugged-looking man at home in the wilderness with a bear as his friend."

Unlike the Hartford campaign in which Earl had been the last resort, Earl was Rod's first choice as a trainer for Hamm's. Rod had been the creator of the B.P. Filling Stations commercials, and he had been impressed with the way Earl and Donna Rae communicated. "He was so gentle with Donna," says Rod. "The two of them seemed to know how to have a good time together. I didn't know if he could work with bears, but I called because he had the quality I wanted. In the beginning, I had no idea of using Earl in the commercials. I only wanted to train a bear so that it could work closely with an actor."

Earl looked at Rod's storyboards and told Rod that while he didn't have a bear then, he was sure he could find one and have it trained in six weeks. He told Rod that his father had kept bears when he was a boy.

"Rod hadn't really thought too much about what kind of bear to use," says Earl. "I told him I thought a black bear was too common, that it had been used too many times before. I suggested using a Kodiak or a grizzly, because they are more distinctive, and I thought they'd photograph well. Rod asked me if I could handle one and I said, 'I don't know.' 'Can you locate one?' I said, 'I think so.' "

Rod told him to try to find the right bear and the agency would advance the money to him so he could buy it. Driving back to New Jersey, Earl felt excited. He liked Rod and trusted him. He liked the idea of working with a big bear. Once at home, he started calling trainers around the country, tapping the grapevine to learn who had bears available.

"I will never take an animal from the wild for an assignment. I always get them either from zoos or other animal trainers. If you work with a wild animal, you spoil him. It's very difficult, if not impossible, to put a wild animal back into the natural environment. There are plenty of animals in captivity. Why add more?"

Earl heard that a man in Calgary, Canada, had a large collection of bears, and rumor had it that he might be willing to sell. The man had tried to put together a movie using bears, but it had fallen through and the man had fourteen bears on his hands.

Liz wanted to go. She had never been that far north. Niki and Jenny had school and she didn't want them to miss it. But a friend was willing to stay with them and Volney could babysit for Mignon.

When they arrived in Calgary, they discovered that the man was just beginning to move into his facilities; everything was in a vaguely chaotic state. "It was like a supermarket of bears," recalls Earl. "The bears were all just sitting there in these unfinished cages. He had several jaguar, but we weren't interested in anything but the bears. I wanted to just take my time and look slowly, but the trainer kept pushing me to jump in and try out the different bears."

"Earl always stands off when he first meets an animal," says Liz. "Some people think he's afraid, but it's his way of showing the animal respect. I know the man in Calgary thought he really couldn't handle bears, that he was frightened. Earl kept walking around, looking at the fourteen bears. He'd stand in front of one of the cages and be silent for nearly half an hour. Then he'd go and stand in front of another one."

"The selection of the right animal is the reason for my success in how they respond," Earl says often. "It's not something I can describe very well. Every animal is an individual. I looked at over 150 stags before I picked Moose. When I walked by the bears in Calgary, I had to try to gauge the chemistry between me and each one. Some were too sluggish and looked as if they didn't want to do anything. Others were too bouncy. Another one says, 'I don't want to work. I'm not your man.' Then all of a sudden something clicks. Here's an animal looking at you, and it says, 'I'll work with you.' You can keep right on walking, and all of a sudden you realize that here's your chance, and you double back."

The animal that caught Earl's eye was called Sasha. He had been born in the Los Angeles Zoo and had spent the first few months of his life in the children's zoo there. Before he was six months old, he had been shipped up to Canada, and since that time he had had little intimate contact with people. Now he was two years old with a thick, golden coat and a distinctive white V on his chest.

Earl pointed him out to Liz, then settled back on his haunches and watched him. The owner came up with a light chain in his hand. "If this is the one you like, why don't you go in with it?" he asked. Earl again shook his head no.

"I always have to give an animal a chance to size up my personality and vice versa before I move in too close. My first impression could be wrong. It may be that the animal and I are really in conflict, and that's a good way to get hurt. Never take anything for granted."

Finally, Earl rose and took the chain from the owner. He opened the door to Sasha's cage and walked in.

Sasha watched and began to wag his head back and forth. His ears, small, round, and erect and set far apart on his broad skull, twitched as Earl took a step closer. His lips rolled back, and he woofed hoarsely. Earl began his sing-song croon: "Oh-h, my-y, what a bootiful bear. . . . I bet you're wondering what I'm doing here. What does that silly-looking man want? I bet you want to know, don't you, don't you?"

Sasha shook his head back and forth, but allowed Earl to put a chain around his neck. Earl stood there for nearly five minutes, talking to Sasha constantly, letting Sasha smell him. Sasha rubbed his nose against Earl's leg. Then Earl gently applied pressure to the chain around Sasha's neck and took a step away. He wanted to see if Sasha would follow. Abruptly, Sasha whipped his head back and forth making violent chomping noises with his jaw. "An informed animal person would know Sasha's warning meant only one thing. I was moving too fast. At that moment, I wondered just how informed I was." Earl took a step back. "The worst thing you can do is to make a sharp movement around any animal—move either slowly or normally. You have to condition yourself to move normally no matter how much you might be in danger, even if the danger is just that you might miss a coffee break, and that's about the level of most of it. If you move either too fast or too slow, the animal will sense that it has you at a disadvantage or at least wonder what you are up to."

As soon as Earl stepped back, Sasha began to

jump up and down. He did not attempt to be aggressive. "I knew then that Sasha wasn't mean. I could tell he was full of fun. I knew he and I were going to have some great times and some bad times, but there was something about Sasha that made me feel he would be worth it, even though he was a hooligan. Was?! Lordy, he still *is* a hooligan! We both are."

Earl walked out of Sasha's cage and told the owner that *she* was the bear he wanted. The owner told Earl he could have the bear, but he had gotten the pronouns mixed up. It was a male, not a female.

Earl shook his head. "From the moment I first went into the cage with Sasha, I began to think of her as female, and I'll never change that. I don't believe it was a conscious decision, but afterward Liz and I talked about it, and I was able to think it out. I knew I didn't want to castrate Sasha. As I've said so many times, I hate to alter an animal, but I knew that if I thought of him as a male, I might try to challenge him. I've got a temper, and in moments of anger it helps me to think of her as female. I would never hit a woman, and while I know Sasha could make mincemeat out of me, I need to have the same attitude toward her as I would toward a woman. I try to tease her out of her moods rather than command her.

"I read somewhere that Gandhi considered teasing part of love. He believed that nonviolence was basically a teasing kind of love. He said he was teasing England into freeing India, as if he were saying, 'Come on, England, I know you don't want to let me starve; I know you have a better nature than the one you are showing.' Sasha has the same power over me, and I have to tease her into accepting me."

After arranging the details of the sale, Earl and Liz went out to celebrate in Calgary. The newest attraction in town was a tower with a nightclub on top from which customers could gaze out at the northern lights. Liz had never seen the northern lights and she convinced Earl to take her to the nightclub. "Earl is afraid of elevators," says Liz, "and you should have seen that man turn white in the elevator. He had stood up to Sasha without flicking an eyelash, but he held on to me in the elevator. He's really frightened of any kind of machine that he has no control over. I think that's why he learned to fly, so he would have a sense of control over an airplane, but he's never gotten over his fear of elevators. He and Mignon."

The next day, Earl arranged to have Sasha flown to Volney's farm. When she arrived, Sasha seemed sluggish and confused by her journey. Earl set up a a training area, a pen seventy feet in diameter, surrounded by a seven-foot-high fence. Then he built a shifting cage for Sasha that measured approximately four feet by eight feet. Sasha would sleep there each night so that she would become accustomed to it. It was important for her to feel at home in the shifting cage for it would be used to transport her when she made commercials.

Earl called Rod and told him he had found a bear. He told Rod that they should choose an actor immediately. The actor would have to come and live at Volney's for six weeks and be a part of the training process from the beginning. Earl told Rod that Sasha's loyalty was not something that could be turned on and off like a faucet. The actor would have to learn to judge Sasha's mood almost as well as Earl himself could, and the actor would have to rely on his own reactions to keep him from danger.

Rod understood Earl's concern and told him to begin training the bear. They would try to decide on an actor and get him to Earl's as soon as possible. Meanwhile, the shooting date for the first series of commercials was set for only six-to-eight weeks away.

The first day, Earl left Sasha completely alone in her shifting cage. The second day, he led her out into the training pen.

"She was still sluggish. She really didn't want to be bothered. The thing about any kind of animal is, you've got to get them to like what they're doing, and it can be difficult.

"I could tell Sasha was not in the mood to be tampered with. I brought our greyhound, Dog, out. At the sight of him, she perked up. She began chasing him around from inside her pen. I don't know what the hell would have happened if they had gotten together. Sasha is as much of a coward as our greyhound, but they both put on a pretty good show. Sasha acted like she really wanted to get at Dog, and Dog acted like he wanted to tear the bear apart. I was glad that he got her moving. I was able to get an idea of what her moods were like and the way she handled herself.

"I didn't try to approach her for five days. I had to learn her body language. I had to learn what the twitch of an ear meant, what she meant when she smiled, when she growled, and when she coughed. She's got a vocabulary you wouldn't believe, and I had to find out quite a bit about her before we could even attempt to communicate."

In *The Little Prince* by Antoine de Saint-Exupéry, the fox teaches the little prince how to tame him. The little prince had never heard the word *tame* and asks the fox what it means. "It means to establish ties," replies the fox. "What must I do to tame you?" asks the little prince. "You must be very patient," replies the fox. "First you will sit down at a little distance from me in the grass. I shall look at you out of the corner of my eye and you will say nothing. Words are the source of misunderstandings. But you will sit a little closer to me every day."

Earl doesn't like the word *tame*, but the definition of "establishing ties" is a very accurate description of the way in which he works.

"After five days, I began to go into the training pen with her. The night before I went in, I didn't give her a full meal. The next day I brought out a smorgasbord of goodies and laid them outside the pen. Sasha could see the food, but she couldn't get at it. It was a bear delicatessen: jelly, honey, marshmallows, fruits, at least half a dozen different kinds of cookies. I fed her a spoonful at a time. It annoyed her because she could see all the food. It taught me an awful lot about her disposition. If you want an animal to follow you, you have to make it realize you are the man with the goodies. Everything the animal does must be rewarded. Sasha can't understand English, so if I wanted her to follow me, I had to make her realize that I was the one with the goodies.

"After Sasha got the idea that I had food with me, I would go in and put a leash on her and then we'd walk. Every time she followed me, she got a marsh-mallow. Then it got so she would run beside me. We'd work forty-five minutes on, ten minutes off, and then repeat the pattern. It depended on her progress. If I pushed her too hard, she'd let me know about it, vocally by her growls and also by her actions. She'd become sluggish, irritable, impatient. Sasha can let me know what she is feeling in a hundred ways. She can go from 'Please let me have a marshmallow, let's take a break' all the way to 'Dammit, I've had enough. You ask me to follow you one more time and I'll cream you.'

"Sasha's paws are her most dangerous weapon. And they play a great role in her language as well. She is saying one thing when they are extended to take a swipe at you and another thing when they are flat. She can hit with a flexed paw or a loose paw; she can deliver a pat, or a barroom roundhouse, or a jab. She can do it all. She favors her right side, and I learned to tell when she was thinking of testing me, but I had to find a way to break her of the habit of using her paws on me. I knew if I didn't she would hurt me someday. As Sasha learned I was her friend, the man who brought her marshmallows, it was natural for her to reach out her paw to me. I want to be around Sasha as long as I possibly can, so I conditioned her to lick my face without putting her paws on me. I never allowed her to place her paws on my shoulder or against my stomach. When she lifted a paw and rested it on my arm affectionately, it was fun and sweet, but I knew that what starts out as an innocent trick can turn out to be a lethal plan. If Sasha got used to putting her paws on me, then

one time when she was really mad she might not
be able to control herself and she'd be so close I
wouldn't have a chance of escaping a real bear hug."

Earl spent hour after hour, putting his cheek out
to Sasha and saying, "Give me a kiss, sweetheart, give
me a kiss." Volney was horrified. It looked to him
as if Earl were indulging in foolish horseplay when
he should be concentrating on the basic rudiments
of discipline. Volney would go inside and complain
to Liz that Earl did not know what he was doing and
would get himself killed.

Yet the kiss became an absolutely crucial part of
Sasha's training. Every time she kissed him without
lifting her paw, she would be rewarded by praise and
a marshmallow. Every time she even lifted her paw
a couple of inches, she would get a sharp reprimand.
After nearly a week, Sasha learned to keep her paws
on the ground or to hold them near her own body.

When Sasha got angry at Earl, she would bite down
on her paw; often in the beginning she would bite
down hard enough to hurt herself. Gradually, as the
training continued, Sasha would only nip at her paw.

Such displacement activity has been observed among
bears in the wild. Two bears challenging each other
will circle slowly. Then, suddenly, as if to relieve the
tension that has been mounting, one bear will tear
at the grass at its feet in vicious gestures.

"Now this is what I mean when I say that I don't
tame Sasha," says Earl. "Sasha's a complex animal. She
might sometimes go into a rage and want unknowingly
to hurt me, but because I am also her friend, she
doesn't. She had to learn how to control her anger.

"Now, if Sasha gets so angry that she really would

bite me, she won't bite as hard as she normally would, because she's used to mouthing her paw instead of chomping down on something. She nips me in anger the way she mouths her paw. She knows the difference between my clothing and my skin. Once she pinched pretty hard, and another time she made me limp for a week, but she didn't break the skin. She just wanted to let me know who was boss."

After Earl and Sasha had been working together for a while, Earl began to carry a pole with him. If Sasha gets out of line, Earl yells, "No, Sasha!" and places the pole in front of her. Sasha has learned to stop at the pole even in anger or frustration. She has learned that if she gets mad she can take it out on the pole. Usually, all she has to do is just pat the pole to make her point. However, once or twice, she's snapped the pole in two just to remind Earl of the kind of strength she has. By the time Earl finished the first commercials there were four Band-Aids on it for a joke.

Of course, there has to be a last defense. It is Sasha's nose, her most sensitive part. Ordinarily, you don't hit a Kodiak bear on the nose; the normal reaction would be violent rage.

"Well," says Earl, "sometimes these things just don't work out according to neat theories. Once or twice I've really thought Sasha was going to have a go at me, and her nose was what was closest for me to hit. If a man were going to hurt you, wouldn't you go for his most sensitive place? So when we have a real showdown, I go for the nose, just a slap of the hand. It's nothing I would recommend to anyone else. I have a glass jaw, but don't tell Sasha."

After about three weeks in the training area, Earl

put Sasha on a fifty-foot nylon leash, and they began taking walks outside the pen. "We'd walk out in the backyard in New Jersey. All the birds would set up a chatter, warning the other animals we were coming. Like all Kodiaks, Sasha loves the water, and I would take her out into the pond. I'd get in a boat, and she would follow me and play in the water. She loved that part of the day. It became a treat for her. Then, later, she'd come out and dry off in the sun, and I actually felt confident enough to relax around her and bask in the sunlight. Once I fell asleep and she woke me up licking my face."

21   Donna Rae poses for an ad.

Donna and Earl check out her new car. **22**

23   Moose eats from Niki's hand.

24 through 28: Sasha's early training.

26

Sasha and Earl on swinging bridge. Sasha to Earl:
"Stop pointing and get us off this thing."

30   Sasha and Earl on solid ground.

Lear Levin getting close-up of Sasha. 31

32   Sasha in motorboat.

33   Sasha and Earl canoeing together in northern Minnesota.

Pushing off with Sasha in a canoe.   34

35   Sasha deciding she'd like to ride in the back of boat with Earl.

Sasha playing with a ball. Rod MacNicholl in background.   (*Right*)

Earl and Sasha sightseeing from a pick-up. (*Right*)   **38**

37   Earl on a horse. Sasha running beside him.

39   Earl and Sasha at ease together.

8

First Commercials
with Sasha

While Earl concentrated on Sasha's early conditioning, the executives at the advertising agency searched for a rugged-looking actor to play the role of Sasha's companion. Many men were available who looked as though they would be comfortable in the outdoors, but none would commit themselves to six weeks of rigorous training with Sasha. The agency was not sure how successful the commercials would be, so they could not promise the actor any more than one series of commercials. Then someone at the agency realized that the perfect solution would be for Earl himself to play the part of the outdoorsman. They asked Earl to come in for a screen test.

"No way," replied Earl. "I'm not going to be an actor." Earl was sure he would be embarrassed and awkward before the cameras, and he had no taste for making a fool of himself.

"People are always making the mistake of thinking

Earl is more sophisticated than he is," says Liz. "They think that Earl's 'shucks, I'm just a country boy' is an act. Even Earl thinks it's an act, but it's not. He's a man with an extraordinary feel for animals, but he is really shy. He wasn't playing hard to get when he said he didn't want to be in the commercials. I'm the opposite. I panic if I'm alone on television or on stage, but if I'm with an animal I can be a ham. When I appeared at the Metropolitan Opera House, I loved every second of it."

The agency asked Earl if he would be willing to allow them to take a few preliminary photographs of him standing next to Sasha. They needed publicity photos to send to the client. Earl agreed. The next day the agency called back. They wanted to know if Earl would come into New York City to have his hair done.

"Done?" queried Earl, who never bothered to go to a barbershop. He wore his beard full and scraggly, and Liz occasionally trimmed his thick brown hair. Earl finally agreed to go to the agency's hairdresser, but reiterated his objections to appearing in the commercials himself. "It's OK," the executives reassured him. "We only need you for some stills, but we will be using a Scandinavian-looking actor, and we want you to be blond."

"My God," Earl recalls. "It took them four hours to 'do' my hair. The man talked about what beautiful hair I had, then he bleached it and bleached it. I tell you, if I had known what I was getting in for, I would have hightailed it out of there like a scared chipmunk."

With his hair and beard trimmed and bleached

blond, Earl posed with Sasha out by the lily pond in front of Volney's farmhouse. The agency and the client were both impressed with how well he photographed. They held a series of meetings to discuss the problem of what to do about an actor. Hamm's Beer wanted the new series of commercials on the air as soon as possible. Earl talked the decision over with Liz, who told him it was too good an opportunity to miss. Earl finally agreed to appear in the commercials, but he insisted on a clause in the contract which stipulated that he be incidental to the action and that the commercials were to concentrate on Sasha.

The first set of commercials was scheduled to be filmed in northern California, and Lief Erikson, a nature photographer and outdoorsman, agreed to work as Earl's assistant with Sasha. Earl arranged for a cargo plane to fly Sasha and himself to California. He packed Sasha into a wooden transport crate that conformed with the airlines' regulation. When he and Lief Erikson arrived at Newark Airport, they discovered that a group of racehorses had been scheduled for the same plane. To the consternation of their trainers, the horses picked up Sasha's scent and broke into a sweat. Horses are particularly sensitive to the danger of bears, and a prolonged trip with Sasha might have ended the careers of the high-strung racehorses.

"Sasha would have loved it," says Earl. "She likes nothing more than stirring up trouble. However, the racehorses had priority. It was a mix-up, and Sasha and I had to wait until another cargo plane was available."

When they arrived in San Francisco, Earl unloaded Sasha from the plane. Because she had been confined to her transport cage an extra day, she seemed nervous. Earl and Lief loaded her into the panel truck that had been rented for her; Earl was anxious to get to the location so that Sasha could rest comfortably.

"That truck was one of the most horrible machines I've ever encountered," Earl remembers bitterly. "It wouldn't steer, and it had bad brakes." Earl had been told the location was a seven-hour drive up the coast, north of San Francisco. For the first hour and a half, the ride was beautiful, with majestic views of the cliffs along the ocean. Then, suddenly, the road turned to gravel.

"I must have made a wrong turn, and we were on a road we shouldn't have come near. I've never been on a road like it. Half the road disappeared down the side of a cliff. It was a miracle we made it. Poor Sasha was moaning and groaning because she was carsick. Lief and I kept the windows open and tried to make her comfortable, but she was crying and sick to her stomach for the whole trip. I let her out to get some air, but as soon as she got back in the truck, she'd be sick again."

The trip took eighteen hours. The nearest town to the location sites was Hyam-Pom, which consisted of a bar, a grocery store, a filling station, a motel, and a sawmill. Sasha and Earl pulled up to the motel around 11:30 at night. "Sasha was so happy to have fresh air again. I think she had spent the entire ride regretting she had ever met me. I took her for a short walk, then bedded her down for the night. We were both exhausted."

Early in the morning, Earl took Sasha out of her cage and led her down the driveway of the motel.

She stopped and rolled back on her haunches. Earl coaxed her to follow him. "She came on," he recalls, "but claws first. She was quick as lightning. She missed me, but I knew she had meant it. I could tell we were in for a tough day. Sasha was not in the mood to be with anybody. She was still feeling tired and sick from the trip." Earl had asked for a couple of days of on-the-job training for Sasha, but since each day cost the client thousands of dollars, they wanted to start work right away. "They just didn't appreciate the fact that a bear's cooperation is not something you can turn on and off like a faucet."

Earl points out that one of the reasons that bears are difficult to train is that they are basically solitary creatures. Unlike Mignon, Sasha has few social instincts. She is inclined to keep to herself. Bears are known for their quick tempers and irritability, and their reputation is well earned.

If Sasha had been born on Kodiak Island, she would have had two years of companionship with her mother, and then she would have spent most of the rest of her life alone. Bear cubs are incredibly helpless at birth, but unlike elephants and higher primates, this vulnerable period is not used to initiate the young into a society.

All through their first summer and fall, the cubs learn from their mother what to eat and how to get it. They learn to tear up the grass to get at tender young shoots, and they practice slapping at stream waters, and during the salmon runs they learn from their mothers the art of fishing.

They bed down with their mother for their first winter, but in the spring she begins to snap at them with increasing ferocity until they learn to leave her alone. From then on, except for brief mating periods, each bear goes its own solitary way. The bear tolerates the presence of other bears at berry time or when salmon are running, but bears do not cooperate with each other, nor do they live in organized families or packs.

Sasha was just a little over two years old when she arrived in California to begin work on the beer commercials. She was at the age when her instincts told her to put an end to intimate contacts. In the wild she would have been ready to leave her mother. Instead, she was being asked to accept the presence not only of Earl, whom at least she knew, but also of a bunch of nervous strangers. Because this was a brand-new advertising campaign, the jobs of many people on this account were dependent on its success. In addition to the production crew, several advertising executives had been flown out from New York to oversee the production. The client had sent a representative, and the hairdresser from New York was paid to keep Earl looking perfect. Altogether, more than a dozen people in various states of anxiety were depending on Sasha to perform well. Of the group, Rod MacNicholl was the only one in whom Earl had confidence. He trusted Rod to help him out with Sasha, knowing how much Rod loves her.

The advertising agency chose Lear Levin to shoot and direct the commercials. Lear is famous for his outdoor commercials, and Earl found him sympathetic. He is tall and lean, with strong muscles in his arms from carrying a camera. Lear studied acting with Uta Hagen, and for most of his commercials, he serves as both director and cameraman. He feels there is a great advantage to the dual role. The actor only has one person to relate to. "When I'm working," he says, "the most important thing I do is to make people feel that one mistake doesn't blow the job. Earl was extremely nervous in California. He didn't know us. It was his first time on camera. It was understandable, but it was tense."

On that first morning of shooting, after her brief show of temper in the driveway, Sasha settled down. Lear decided to start with an easy shot. Earl and Sasha were to walk through some mossy rocks at a leisurely pace. Earl carried a pouch full of semimoist dog food, marshmallows, and Holloway Milk Duds, good because the caramel centers took Sasha a long time to finish. Earl hadn't fed Sasha breakfast so that she would be hungry enough to follow him for her reward. As Earl walked, he fed Sasha bits of food and the shot went perfectly.

By midmorning, Lear decided to try to film a scene in which Sasha followed Earl across a log. In the forest north of Hyam-Pom, Lear had found a beautiful thick log that rested across a twenty-five foot gully. A muddy stream ran along the bottom. Earl and Rod had discussed the scene; Earl and Sasha had practiced walking across a log in New Jersey, and Sasha had shown no fear.

Lear set up his cameras beneath the log. The advertising executives and the client huddled around the cameras offering suggestions. Earl and Sasha waited up on the hill with Lief Erikson and Rod MacNicholl on either side of Sasha. It took forty-five minutes for the cameras to be put completely into focus. Meanwhile, Earl fed Sasha three boxes of Milk Duds to keep her happy. Her hunger had lost its edge, and she was beginning to get bored. Earl hoped they'd be able to get the shot off before her attention span was gone for good.

Finally, everybody was ready, and the assistant cameraman shouted, "Action!" Earl snapped off Sasha's leash and started to stride across the log. In his hand, hidden from the camera, he held a marshmallow. Halfway across the log, Earl realized Sasha was not following him. She was sitting on the edge of the log, playing with the loose bark, using her long claws to dig for bugs and worms. Earl called to her, but she didn't bother to lift her head. Finally, Rod gave her a gentle nudge on the backside, just touching her hair. Sasha bounded across the log. Lear asked for another take, which went well, but just to cover the shot, they needed one more.

Sasha started across, and the bark on the log twisted under her weight. She lost her grip and went careening into the gully. She uttered a sharp cry of surprise and tried to claw her way back to safety. She rolled on her left shoulder, did a somersault, and came to her feet, making a tremendous whooshing sound as she rose. She shook her head back and forth furiously, her jaws hanging loose to reveal her sharp incisors.

Someone yelled, "Take off! The bear's loose!"

Earl yelled, "That's a good way to get killed. Stand still!"

Sasha took three jumps toward the camera. Earl was perched twelve feet above on the log. There was no way he could get down to Sasha fast enough if she decided to attack. Everybody except the hairdresser and Lear began to run down the gully toward the stream bed.

The first man jumped the tiny runoff and made it up the side of the road. Fast on his heels came the Hamm's Beer representative from Minnesota. He was an average man, about thirty pounds overweight, his face turned bright red from the exertion, and his arms flailing about wildly. Stumbling down the hill, his glasses flew from his face, but he didn't stop to pick them up. As he readied himself to jump across the stream, he looked back to see if the bear was following him. Sasha was not in sight, but as he explained later, he could hear the sounds of something thrashing through the undergrowth. It was the assistant cameraman who was running with *his* head turned around to see if *he* was about to be eaten!

In true slapstick tradition, the assistant cameraman plowed into the man from Minnesota, knocking him face forward into the bottom of the gully. Then the cameraman proceeded to run right over him, stepping first on the client's leg, then onto his back, and finally on his head.

Meanwhile, the wild beast that had caused the panic was standing still, shaking her head back and forth. Earl slipped down the gully and snapped on her leash. Sasha rubbed her head against his leg. "She was just like a little kid who couldn't understand what had happened to her. The last thing on her mind was attacking someone. She had had the wind knocked out of her, and she was looking for someone to come and make everything all right."

Once Earl made sure that Sasha wasn't hurt, he surveyed the scene in front of him and burst out laughing. "The only one standing still was the hairdresser, just taking it all in. I tell you my respect for that guy went up a thousand percent. Up by the log, Rod Mac-Nicholl had a big frown on his face, which is normal, but his eyes were dancing, dancing, dancing. To this day, Sasha has held a grudge against Rod because she thinks he was responsible for pushing her off the tree and he never touched her."

Earl and Rod stopped laughing when they learned the client had developed a huge knot on the back of his foot. Usually the client is the most pampered person on the set. Certainly, he is the last one anybody would want to step on. He was bundled back to the motel, propped up with pillows, and plied with martinis. His ankle was only slightly sprained. "I never felt too bad about it," says Earl. "He recovered and I'm sure he has a good time telling his story about the time the bear *almost* got him."

When Earl arrived back in Hyam-Pom with the injured client, he discovered that rumors of an accident on the set had become extremely elaborate. "The story had leaked out that the bear had turned on its trainer. I swear they had started to form a posse to shoot the bear. I don't know where they got the news —maybe by the tom-toms of Hyam-Pom."

After the client had been made comfortable, Lear wanted to continue working. There were still several hours of daylight left, and he wanted to take advantage of it. He conferred with Earl, who agreed to try a simple shot of Sasha following Earl along the banks of the Trinity River.

Sasha was not cooperative.

"She didn't want to work, she wanted to play, but very slowly—she was still feeling the effects of having had the wind knocked out of her. She would take a few steps and then stop, her eyes sparkling. She would grin and laugh about fifteen feet away from me and jump up and down. I couldn't blame her for wanting to play. She had been carsick and had fallen off the log. Lear was very patient. He would run the cameras and get the few shots he could, but she was not in the mood to do anything but play."

Finally, Earl decided to let her romp in the Trinity River. The spray and the noise delighted Sasha. She slapped the water with her paws and laughed when it hit her on the nose. She didn't know how to balance herself on the slippery rocks, and she made a game out of falling into the water, picking herself up, and plunging in again.

At the end of the day, Earl treated Sasha to a ride in a jeep back to the motel. He had taught her to ride in a jeep back in New Jersey. He would put food in the front seat, and when Sasha saw the marshmallows she would climb in. She was startled by the noise of the engine, but she soon learned to love jeep rides, hanging over the windshield so the wind could blow in her face.

On their way to town, Earl and Sasha passed a woman on a motorcycle. A six-year-old boy was seated behind her, his arm stretching to reach around her waist. "I had never seen a woman ride a big Harley 500 before, much less with a little kid on the back. I don't think she had ever seen a bear riding in an open jeep. We both did double takes. She almost went over the edge. She made a big U turn and came barreling back to take another look. Then we both waved and laughed."

The next day Lear suggested filming some scenes of Sasha in the jeep. He wanted a shot of Sasha sitting in the front seat of the jeep, looking at a group of cows in a pasture. Sasha kept looking at the camera instead of at the cows. Lear yelled to Earl, "Get her to look the other way."

"Of course, at the sound of his voice, she turned toward him," says Earl. "Lear was much more interesting to look at than some cows. I tried to get her to do what he wanted. I kept pointing at the cows and saying, 'Look, Sasha, look.'

"I felt as if she was saying to me, 'But the camera's over there, Earl . . . we're making a movie. I don't have time to look at cows. I wish you would shut up, you're incidental. I'm the star.' "

Finally, Lear got the shot he wanted. Sasha started leaning over the windshield looking at the cows. However, she leaned a little too far and fell out. Earl was only going about ten miles an hour. Sasha jumped up, then ran toward the car. "Oh, it was a merry chase," recalls Earl. "She turned it into a game. She kept running in smaller and smaller circles until finally I got her by jumping out of the jeep. She was tired of playing and ready for work again."

With only six weeks of training behind her, Sasha was very unpredictable, and Lear learned to shoot around her moods. If she took a few steps in the right direction, he would shoot quickly, knowing she might not be in the mood to take those steps again. However, some shots were absolutely necessary. Each commercial had to end with scenes of Earl drinking beer, and Rod had to dream up different settings.

One scene took place in a logging camp. Bona fide loggers had been hired as extras, and they made fun of Earl's retinue of hairdressers and makeup men. "I'm not used to that kind of attention," says Earl. "I told the makeup man, 'Get that big son of a bitch up there, the one who's giving me all the trouble. Get him down here and powder his nose.' So my friend called him down and put pancake makeup all over him, and then everyone razzed *him*. Then he knew how I felt."

When they were ready to shoot, Earl brought Sasha onto the set. The loggers showed their respect for Sasha immediately by sitting high up out of her way. Earl spotted a big pile of wood chips, turned to Lear, and said, "Let Sasha loose in those wood chips and you'll have yourself a beautiful shot." Sasha fell into the wood chips, rolling in them over and over. Lear shot nearly six minutes' worth of film. "The problem with a commercial," explains Earl, "is that it is so short. They used about five seconds of that six minutes. In California they shot 28,000 feet of film for the commercials they shot and they ended up using 90 feet per commercial. But I felt good about the shot in the wood chips."

The motto of Hamm's Beer is "from the land of the sky blue waters," referring to the northern Minnesota lake country. The client considered one commercial essential—a shot of Earl in a canoe on a lake with Sasha swimming beside him. Earl anticipated no problem with this commercial. He had studied it on the storyboard; it called for him and Sasha to walk to the edge of the lake, and then for him to get into the canoe and call for Sasha to come in for a swim beside him. "She loves to swim. I practiced that shot about a dozen times at Volney's, and she'd swim beside me in Volney's pond."

Unfortunately, there were no lakes near Hyam-Pom. Sasha loved to play in the clear and sparkling Trinity River, but the river did not look like northern Minnesota. The only body of water that resembled a lake was a large yellowish green pond. Lear studied it and told the executives it would not be a problem to shoot the pond with the proper filters so that it would look sky blue.

The pond had a murky, mossy bottom, perfect for the breeding of bullhead fish. Every time the merest ripple hit the pond, bullheads would rise to the surface and gulp for air.

Lear set up his cameras on the shore of the pond and told Earl to lead Sasha slowly into the water. Dressed in his leather jacket and carrying his pole, Earl strode to the pond with Sasha beside him. Sasha put one paw into the water, and a dozen bullheads flipped in front of her. She gave Earl a startled look and bolted. Earl caught up with her and tried to calm her down. Eventually, Sasha allowed him to lead her back to the pond. Tentatively, she stuck her paw back into the water. It was so murky she could not see the bottom.

"She was like a child who won't go in because the bottom's icky. I waded into the pond up to my waist and held marshmallows out to her, but she didn't want anything to do with that pond. I yelled at her, but nothing I could do would make her go in. She was beginning to get angry and frustrated, and I wanted her to relax, so I tied her up in the woods a little bit away from the pond and we tried to figure out what to do."

John Brown, a local resident, had been watching the proceedings from the sidelines. "You're going to get yourself killed, treatin' that bear like a playmate," he volunteered. While the executives talked with Lear about what would happen if they could not get a picture of Sasha swimming in a lake, John Brown took Rod aside.

"I've got an idea how we could get that bear into the water," he said. He had everyone gather twenty sturdy logs and fashioned them together into an impromptu raft, which they floated onto the pond. Earl poured a bottle of Hamm's Beer on the deck, christening it the S.S. *John Brown*.

They tied a long rope to one end of the raft. Earl explained John Brown's plan to Lear and then got Sasha. She was in a much better mood, and she followed him to the edge of the pond, but once there she shook her head back and forth as if to say, "Oh, no, not this again."

Earl stepped onto the raft and urged Sasha to follow him. Gingerly, Sasha put part of her weight onto the raft. It sank an inch or two, but it supported her. As soon as she had all four paws on the raft, Earl jumped into the water and gave the raft a shove with all his strength. It drifted onto the pond.

Earl got into a canoe next to the raft. Holding onto Sasha's leash, he yelled to the crew onshore to start pulling the rope attached to the raft. Like bargemen on the Volga, they pulled their 600-pound cargo out into the middle of the pond. As the raft made its slow path through the murky water, bullheads flipped on top of the raft. "I kept talking to her, reassuring her the bullheads couldn't hurt her. It was ludicrous —a 600-pound Kodiak frightened of some tiny bull-heads."

When Sasha was out in the middle of the pond, Lear focused his cameras directly on her. An assistant shouted, "Action!" At the signal, John Brown and the crew gave three sharp tugs on the rope. As John Brown had predicted, the raft flipped over, tumbling Sasha into the pond. She tried to scramble back onto the raft, but John Brown's crew hauled it out of her reach. Earl maneuvered his canoe next to her so that through Lear's camera it looked as if Sasha was enjoying a swim. "Goddam, that was the hardest shot we ever got," says Earl. "Here it was supposed to look like the two of us enjoying a day on the water, and Sasha was swimming for all she was worth because she just hated that pond. When she reached the shore, Lear got a beautiful long-distance shot of Sasha jumping up and down. In the commercials, she looks as if she is in a good mood . . . jumping for sheer joy. In reality, she was jumping because she was glad to feel something solid under her feet. God, what a day. John Brown couldn't believe what we were doing with her—running around with her in a jeep, flipping her off rafts. He said to me, 'I know what those bears can do to you. You're going to get it one of these days.' "

Earl drove Sasha back to town. He could tell from the way she paced up and down in her cage that she was still upset over her ordeal on the raft. "I didn't want to break her trust in me. If I played too many tricks on her, it would ruin our relationship. I don't think we did anything cruel to her—once she started swimming, she really didn't mind—but still she had had a hard day, so had we all.

"I took her down to the Trinity River and let her play in the cool water. We were all alone, just the two of us, and I had to laugh. Fifteen men had spent nearly six hours trying to figure out a way to get her to swim. Now, with no one watching, Sasha was swimming like a fish. In fact, I had a hard time getting her out of the water. There was a strong current, and I was afraid she might be swept downstream, but she loved it."

The next morning, Sasha had another ordeal to face. Lear had discovered a swinging bridge overlooking a deep gorge. It was a spectacular sight, and Lear believed that if he could get a shot of Earl and Sasha on the bridge it would add beauty and drama to the commercial. Surprise shots such as these made his commercials prizewinners.

It was a cold, crisp morning, the type of weather Sasha likes best. Earl loaded her into the panel truck and drove to the site of the swinging bridge. The early morning fog had settled in the lower reaches of the gorge, and the bridge swayed above, held by cables, two on top and two on the bottom. Logs had been slashed onto the cables, and the boards nailed on top of the logs. The bridge sagged in the center and looked highly precarious.

Sasha came bounding out of the truck. She followed Earl up the incline to the start of the bridge. He could hardly hold her back—she was in the mood to run and play. When they got to the gorge, the wind was blowing and the whole bridge was swaying. Lief Erikson got on one side of the bridge and Rod on the other. Sasha was hungry. She hadn't had any breakfast, and she knew the only way to get any goodies was to follow Earl onto the bridge. Earl took a few steps, and Sasha walked halfway out. Then she would turn and run for the side. Rod stood at the entrance of the bridge with a pole barring her way. "She was really of two minds," says Earl. "Part of her just wanted to get the hell off that bridge, but on the other hand she didn't want to leave me because I'm the big daddy and she thinks I'm supposed to protect her."

After Lear got the shot he needed, Rod backed away so that Earl and Sasha could get off the bridge. Sasha walked past Rod very calmly. Rod turned and took a few steps in front of her. He was carrying a small knapsack over his shoulder. As soon as he had turned away from her, Sasha grabbed the knapsack, and before anyone knew what was happening, she rummaged through it and ate Rod's wallet, including all his credit cards. Earl laughed so hard tears streamed down his face. "She really knew exactly how to get to him where it hurt—just chewed up his American Express card. She got him back for pushing her off that log, and damn it, he never touched her. She was blaming him for something he had never done."

The last commercial in the series called for Earl and Sasha to fish on the bank of the river. On the storyboards, Rod had pictured Sasha with a fish in her mouth. Earl thought it would make a beautiful commercial, but he explained to Rod that if they wanted to show Sasha catching a fish they would have to find extremely shallow water. Young bears do not know how to hook fish with their claws; they can only catch fish when the fish's back is actually out of water. Only after much experience do they learn to spot the quick dart of a fish in water.

Sasha was not only a young bear, she had never tried to fish in her life or watched another bear fish. Her one experience with fish in the wild had been with the bullheads on the raft. Earl told Rod and Lear that the water had to be only one or two inches deep or Sasha would not be able to catch a fish.

The crew found a beautiful site where the Trinity River rushed by a gravel bed. The water varied from six feet to six inches. They bought thirty live trout from a nearby hatchery, and the crew erected chicken wire barriers below and above the spot that Lear wanted to film. Sasha would have thirty captive trout to choose from.

Earl brought Sasha down to the stream, took one look at the six inches of water, and said, "It won't work."

No one understood. "The water looked shallow to them, but six inches was too deep. It didn't matter how many fish they had trapped—Sasha would not be able to see them.

"Yet Lear and Rod and the others were sure it would work. They couldn't understand that four inches would make a big difference. Sometimes an animal man has a hard time communicating. They told me to stop worrying and made me sit in the middle of the stream on a log overhanging the water. I had to sit there like an idiot trying to figure out what to do with myself."

Sasha waded into the water. Her efforts were comical and ineffectual—she slapped at the water and snapped at the spray, but caught no fish. The violent movements of the fish startled her each time she got close enough to make a catch. Her paws would be inches from a fish, but as soon as it flitted its quick tail, Sasha would shake her head back and forth and miss. It was as if some instinct told her that this was a familiar activity, but she had no idea of how to go about it. The trout would disappear into the deeper water, and Sasha would give up.

Earl instructed the crew to throw the fish right at Sasha. The crew scrambled into the water, struggling to catch the slippery trout in their bare hands. They had as much trouble as Sasha. Finally, they got a net and caught quite a few. They threw the fish in graceful high arcs so Sasha would have plenty of time to watch their descent. The fish landed right at Sasha's feet. She dived after each throw, understanding exactly what was expected of her, but the fish blended so well with the water that she lost them.

Suddenly one of the fish landed right on top of her paw. Whether by accident or design, she lifted her paw and caught the trout's fleshy back. The trout squirmed, and Sasha bent her head down and grabbed it in her mouth. She looked up, and Earl caught her eye.

"She was so proud and tickled that she got the fish. I waved to her to come out to me. She splashed across the water with the fish still in her mouth. She rose up and put her big front paws on the log I was sitting on. She was like a big golden retriever. It was nothing we could have planned, and they got it all on film. She wanted to show me her catch. I think that it was one of the proudest moments of my life—the fact that we were getting that close, such good friends that she wanted me to share her success."

That night, Earl called Liz to tell her how well the shooting was going. He felt on top of the world. The trip to California and the success with the commercials had made him realize how much he craved a place of his own. "The clean river, the mountains, the fresh air—I wanted a beautiful place like that for Liz, the kids, and myself. I called Liz and said, 'Honey, if you want me back, you'd better start looking for a place of our own. 'Cause I'm not coming back to that swamp.' And she knew I wasn't kidding."

9

Back at Volney's

Liz was not surprised by the feeling Earl expressed in his phone call. Earl had often talked of moving. It was late February. Soon Mignon would be a year old, and she would need larger quarters.

Over the months, Mignon had changed the apartment drastically. As she developed power in her trunk, one by one the house decorations had come crashing down. "Nothing she did was purposefully destructive," says Liz. "It was just that she was developing so much power.

"I hardly noticed the changes; they happened gradually. For example, she loved to scratch her behind on a huge heavy oak buffet in the dining room. Then one day, she rubbed against it, and sent it flying across the room.

"She loved the cold frost on the window. She'd rub on the window with her lip where her trunk went into her mouth. As she got bigger, she broke all the windows one by one, and we had to replace them with plexiglass."

By the time Mignon was six months old, Liz had started her on solid foods and her weight increased almost geometrically, averaging a gain of about 100 pounds a month. Liz fed her every fruit and vegetable she could buy and gave her a wide choice of breads—rye, whole wheat, oatmeal, white, and pumpernickel.

"I did spoil her," Liz admits. "It was a long time before I would give her any animal food. I thought she could eat what we ate, and she agreed with me. She wouldn't even eat the skins of bananas because we didn't. We wanted her to eat the skin because it has nutritional value, but she learned to peel bananas by herself. She would hold a banana between her two front feet and peel it with her trunk. She even learned to peel apples. She cost us a fortune to feed, nearly $25 a day. The only thing she would not eat was peanuts. She hated peanuts, and people were always trying to give them to her."

Before he left for California, Earl insisted that they start to feed Mignon hay. In the wild, grasses would make up the substantial bulk of her diet. Earl put a couple of handfuls of hay into Mignon's feed pan. Mignon refused to eat it. She flung it around the room as if it were confetti. "I sat and tried to figure out how to make hay resemble something that she liked," recalls Liz. "She loved salad with salad dressing, so I cut about a dozen tomatoes into little pieces, snipped the hay into one-inch sections, then mixed in cucumbers and lettuce, and poured Wishbone salad dressing over the whole thing."

Mignon picked out the lettuce, cucumbers, and

tomatoes; carefully sucked out all the dressing; and left the hay. It sat in the bottom of the bowl in a soggy lump. Liz decided she was not going to persist in cutting hay into tiny sections and pouring gallons of dressing in it, and Mignon did not try hay again until she was well over a year old.

Throughout the first year, Liz continued to give Mignon a half-gallon baby bottle every hour, day and night. Mignon went through a case of evaporated milk each day. Liz learned to sleep deeply in between feedings. Despite waking up every hour through the night, she did not find herself particularly tired or drained. "You fall into a rhythm and you get used to it. People were always asking me how I could stand getting up every hour and putting up with all the disruptions in my life that Mignon caused, but it didn't bother me. The thrill of having Mignon gave me more energy than I normally would have had. I loved watching her develop. Every time her trunk got a little stronger, it was as thrilling to me as if I were watching my own child in its first year. The excitement of watching Mignon's intelligence grow was great for Earl and me. We learned so much— exactly how adaptable elephants are and how sensitive they can be to nuances of emotion. It was such a pleasure, also, to watch Mignon with Niki and Jenny. The three could communicate on a level that I have never seen with another animal. I felt we were very privileged to have the opportunity to learn so much both from and about Mignon that it was worth the expense and it was worth the disruption of our lives."

One of Liz's most poignant memories was her first New Year's Eve with Mignon. Earl was in California. By the time she was nine months old, Mignon weighed 700 pounds. New Year's Eve was a rainy, foggy night, more like April than December. Volney's leg was still hurting from the fall during the flood. He had stayed inside all day, and Liz and two friends did all the chores. Niki and Jenny were spending the holiday with their grandparents.

For the first time in six weeks, Volney felt well enough to cook his specialty, baked beans. Liz had a few friends in for a round of drinks, and all left before midnight. Mike and Dandelion, the two lion cubs, were still in the house. Liz turned on the television to watch Guy Lombardo usher in 1973 at the Waldorf Astoria. Mignon pushed her rocker in front of the set and settled into it. Mildred, a Macaw, perched on Volney's shoulder. Volney had taught Mildred to say, "I can talk, can you fly?" Luther the owl sat on the bookcase above the television set. Dog lay down at Liz's feet. Dandelion lay curled between Mignon's feet, and Mike jumped onto Liz's lap.

"There I was, a shot of Old Grand-Dad in my glass, watching Mignon sitting in her rocker with the lion cub between her legs. I remember thinking to myself, 'You're the luckiest person in the world. You'd better remember this year, because you'll never have another one like it.' "

Two months later, Liz received Earl's phone call telling her to look for a farm. She had been about to take Moose up to board at a game farm in north-western Pennsylvania. He would be healthier grazing on grass than he would eating hay on Volney's small farm.

Liz's friend Paula Nowak, who bred Arabian horses, agreed to accompany her. Paula wanted to visit Callenburger's farm on Route 15 in central Pennsylvania. Callenburger owned Surf, a legendary Arabian stallion. Liz piled Niki and Jenny into the car and hitched Moose's trailer to the back.

"I'll never forget our arrival at Callenburger's. We drove in with Moose in the trailer, and Mr. Callenburger brought Surf over to our car so Paula could see him. Surf started strutting and snorting, glad-eyeing the trailer. He thought that anything that showed up in a trailer was a mare for him. He looked over the top of the trailer, and there was a huge stag. He did the closest thing to a double take that I've ever seen a horse do. He actually gawked. 'Antlers!? What am I supposed to do with this?' Paula and I practically bent over double laughing."

Later, Liz drove higher into the Alleghenies. As the hills stretched out beneath them, Liz felt they were traveling to the top of the earth. She turned to Paula and said, "It's so beautiful. It would be a perfect place for us to live."

In a local newspaper Liz discovered an advertisement for a 500-acre farm in Tioga, Pennsylvania. She called the real estate agent and told them that as soon as her husband returned from California, they would like to come up and look at the farm.

The day that Earl and Sasha arrived home, it rained constantly. Between thundershowers, Earl helped Volney shift animals in order to repair cages. Since

Volney's animals were not tame, coaxing them into temporary cages was always difficult, particularly in the rain. In the evening, Liz and Earl took off for Pennsylvania to look at the property.

They arrived at dawn. The farm consisted of 525 acres of rolling hills. Beyond the house, the pastures turned into woods crisscrossed with deer paths that led to two large beaver ponds. The barns had been built solidly, but they had deteriorated and needed work. The main farmhouse was simple, but had six bedrooms. After a lifetime of apartment living, Liz gloried in the thought of having guest bedrooms. Less than a quarter of a mile up the road, there was a second, smaller house that they could perhaps rent.

"The farm gave us both a strange feeling," says Liz. "We were not quite sure what the feeling meant . . . whether it was good luck . . . or if it meant we should stay away. Perhaps we were a little afraid of the commitment. We told the agent we had to think about it."

On the drive back to Volney's, Earl and Liz discussed what the move would mean. In many ways, it was an ideal location. Only five hours from New York, they would be close enough to come into the city for conferences with advertising agencies. The countryside was beautiful. The only thing that worried them was the possibility of flooding. Western Pennsylvania had been badly hurt by Hurricane Agnes, and while the owner assured them the farm was far above the flooding plain, they were both afraid of buying a place that was susceptible to floods. They decided to pick a very rainy day and drive up to the farm again.

Two days after their return, Moira the lioness gave birth to a second family, and Volney named them Liz and Earl. This time, Moira was able to nurse, and Liz didn't bring them into the house. A few days later, it rained all day and through the night. Liz and Earl, humans, not the lion cubs, decided that it would be a good day to take a second look at the farm. Once again, they arrived at dawn, but this time with Niki and Jenny in tow. They walked around the farm in the rain, and although they discovered many underground springs in the pastures, they saw that there was very good drainage. They walked back to the house to find that another family had arrived from New Jersey and was about to buy the farm. The owner told Liz and Earl that they had first option, but they would have to decide right away. The other family was willing to give him a check then and there.

"We hardly even took a second to decide," recalls Liz. "We looked at each other, and then I wrote a check. My hand was shaking, but we finally had our own home."

Liz and Earl agreed to give the owners of the farm time to find another place to live. After making the preliminary arrangements for a mortgage, Liz and Earl and the children drove back to Volney's. They arrived back exhausted, but happy to report that they had bought a 525-acre farm.

Every few weeks, Liz called the owners of the farm to ask if they had found a place; the answer was always no.

"They were very nice people," says Liz. "And we knew that they loved the hills of the farm, but it had just become too big a property for them to keep up. It occurred to us that the perfect solution would be to let them keep a piece of the property and build their own house on it. They were very happy with the idea and moved into a little trailer while their house was being built so that we could start moving in."

Nonetheless, it wasn't until the beginning of August that Liz and Earl were ready to move. As they began to pack, the rains started. Earl took the first load of their household things up in the rain. While he was gone, Liz continued to pack. The rains filled Volney's lowest pond until it overflowed, reaching the back of the snake house. Liz finished the packing with visions of having to interrupt it in order to move Volney's animals once again. Although another couple was moving into the apartment to help Volney with the work, Liz didn't want to leave him in the midst of another flood. Earl came back from Pennsylvania and took up another load. The water leveled off and remained stationary all day. During the night the water receded, and Liz packed all through the night.

Finally, on August 7, they were ready to leave. It required a veritable caravan to move all the animals, equipment, and people. Earl was in the lead with his twenty-seven-foot horse trailer packed with every conceivable type of animal equipment. Liz followed in the minibus with Niki and Jenny in the front seat, and Mignon in the back with Luther the owl and Robert the bobcat. Joe Nowak followed Liz in his horse trailer filled with barnyard animals, and Steve McAuliff brought up the rear, his Ford convertible packed to overflowing with more household things. Earl started his motor at 3:00 P.M., and they pulled out. Volney waved good-bye. Later that night, he would write in his diary:

> *Liz moved here the last week of April 1965, and it's been a happy experience having her. It's still my belief she's the best person Lorraine D'Essen of Animal Talent Scouts developed, and we wish her and her family, animals and humans, much happiness.*

The ride to Tioga was long and tiring. Earl had such a heavy load in the trailer that he could not go over 40 mph. Most of the trip was made in darkness. At about eleven o'clock at night, when they were about five miles away from Tioga, the headlights of the minibus shorted and went out. With Earl in front of her and Joe Nowak behind her, Liz felt she was in little danger and decided to drive on. All oncoming cars would see Earl's lights, and any car that wanted to pass would see the rear lights of Steve McAuliff and Joe Nowak.

Just as they were within one hundred yards of the dirt road that led to the farm, Liz heard a siren. A policeman pulled her over to the side of the road and began shouting at her as he emerged from his car. He told Liz he had been following her with his lights flashing for two miles and wanted to know why she hadn't pulled over. As he questioned her, he waved his flashlight around the minibus suspiciously. Liz started to laugh.

"I couldn't help myself. I told him I hadn't seen his flashing light because there was a ton of elephant blocking my rear view, but his mind wouldn't register what I was saying. His light kept shining on Mignon, but I swear he never saw that there was an elephant in the back seat. He acted as if he hadn't heard me. He didn't even say, 'Cut the joke. What elephant?' He kept threatening to give me a ticket. Finally, I convinced him that we'd be all right for the mile or two we had left, and he let us go. When we got to the farm, we were all so exhausted that after getting fresh water for the animals we fell asleep in the cars."

In the morning, they inspected the house and barns and realized Mignon would have to be put in the barn. She was getting too big to live in the house, but Liz didn't want to put her in the barn permanently. Earl promised to build Mignon a pen in the basement of the farm house, and it seemed the best immediate solution. She would be close enough so that she could hear the sounds of the family, and it would be easy for them to go down to visit her.

Earl suggested that Liz let Mignon sleep by herself in the barn until her pen was ready. "I've always been convinced," he says rather wearily, "that the damn elephant could sleep alone."

"She was still a baby. I wasn't going to leave her all by herself," replies Liz. "I was sure she would be scared."

Earl decided that if Liz wanted to sleep outside with her elephant she could, but he had just bought a house and he wanted to sleep in it. He told Liz she could sleep with Mignon in the big trailer.

Although she is not afraid of elephants, coyotes, wolves, or badgers, Liz does not like to go out in the dark alone. Each night she convinced either Niki or Jenny to join her in a sleeping bag out by the trailer. "I tried to pretend it was a great adventure, but they wanted to sleep in the new house in their own bedroom. They really did not enjoy being dragged out of bed to sleep with Mommy and Mignon in a trailer. One night it rained. The trailer not only leaked, but the noise of the rain on the roof was like torture. Niki and I came running back to the house soaking wet."

Finally, Liz convinced Earl to sleep in the barn with her and Mignon. "I've never been good at putting my foot down," admits Earl. "Liz gets me laughing and the next thing I know I've agreed to one of her crazy schemes. That's how we got the elephant in the first place."

They put a double mattress on the earth floor of the barn. At first, they left Mignon loose because she liked to put her trunk on the sleeping couple to reassure herself that they were there. Then Mignon decided that she didn't like sleeping on hay.

"The whole idea of staying in the barn did not appeal to her," says Liz. "She really didn't believe that elephants belonged in barns. She started to rip our pillows out from under our heads and throw them around the barn. When we got up to retrieve our pillows, she threw hay at us. Finally, we got so annoyed that we tied her up and moved our bed far enough away so she couldn't reach us. I would wake up in the middle of the night and go play with her and give her a bottle."

Liz found she loved sleeping in the barn. In the early morning they could open the back door and watch the fog come in. Earl has no comment.

They slept in the barn all through September and part of October while Earl fabricated a heavy metal pen for Mignon in the basement.

By the beginning of October, it had started to get cool at night. Liz and Earl put up heat lamps for Mignon and covered her with two blankets. In the middle of October, Liz went to Boston with Niki and Jenny to visit her parents.

While she was away, Earl moved Mignon into her new basement home. The first night, when she trumpeted, Earl went down with a bottle for her and explained to her firmly that she was going to have to sleep by herself. "If Liz was home and heard her hollering and complaining, she'd move us both to the basement. I knew that Mignon would get used to it after a few nights, and by the time Liz came home, Mignon was all settled in and seemed to accept it as home."

When Liz got back from Boston, she rushed to the basement to visit Mignon. "Earl hadn't given her a bed, so I made her one out of cinder blocks and plywood, just like the one we had for her in New Jersey. I put a mattress on top of it, and every morning when I came down to give her breakfast, she had thrown the mattress outside the pen. Being a good Jewish mother, I kept throwing it back in, and she kept heaving it out. Finally, months later I figured she didn't want a bed anymore. I think it was her way of telling me that she was growing up."

10

Sasha and Horses

One of the reasons Earl was anxious to get Mignon settled as quickly as possible was that he and Sasha were scheduled to do another series of commercials for Hamm's Beer. The first commercials were aired in late spring of 1973, and they drew a very positive response. Hundreds and then thousands of fan letters were sent to Hamm's headquarters in Minneapolis. People wrote that they had never enjoyed a commercial more—that the commercials were far better than anything else on television. They wanted to know more about the Hamm's man and his bear. Were they really friends? Where did they live? What did they do when they weren't on television? Neither the agency nor Hamm's had expected such a response. Within months, the commercials had increased the sale of beer and the client was even more pleased. By midsummer, Hamm's had ordered a new set of commercials to be shot in the fall. These commercials were to be filmed in northern

Minnesota in the heart of the famous Boundary Waters Canoe area at the end of Minnesota's Gunflint Trail.

When Earl heard a new series was being created, he and Rod held a conference. "I could tell they were excited, and I knew from experience that we had to capitalize on the fact that we were hot. Advertising campaigns are so unpredictable; you can never tell when they are going to go cold on you. I appreciated having another chance to work with a company I respected, and to be an image for a product that I liked. I said to Rod, 'Let's give it everything we've got. Let's come up with something really unusual.' We kicked around a lot of ideas. Then I suggested using horses and Sasha in one commercial of the new series."

Rod thought such a commercial would be beautiful, *if* it could work. Horses are notoriously afraid of bears. It can take a trainer six months to get a horse to accept a *dead* bear across its back. It is correspondingly more difficult to train a horse to work with a live bear. The storyboard Rod and Earl worked up depicted Earl on a pack trip astride one horse and leading another. Sasha was to run alongside. The commercials evoked the image of a mythic mountain man of the West.

As soon as they had moved up to Tioga, Earl began preparing Sasha for the commercials. "She had never been around other animals. She and I could work together, but I was concerned about how she would react to horses. Would she try to bluff them? Would she try to play with them? Or would she become aggressive?"

At first, Earl could not get any of his horses to go

within fifty feet of her cage. However, he had his old Tibetan pony that had been with him for years. According to Earl, she was a horse with more guts than any other animal on the farm. "She's like a snooping auntie. She's just got to stick her nose into whatever is happening." Earl led Tibet up to Sasha's cage. Sasha could smell her through the fence, and started jumping up and down and shaking her head back and forth. Tibet's legs stiffened, and for the first time she showed fright.

"Sasha's such a hooligan," says Earl. "She knew old Tibet was scared. She sat back on her haunches with a big smile on her face as if to say, 'Come on, I just want to be friends.' She gets what I call her 'suckering-them-in look.' If Sasha had been born a human, I swear she would be a success on Madison Avenue. In fact, it's probably no accident that she did end up in advertising."

Sasha sat back and waited for Tibet's nerve to return. Old Tibet looked at her dubiously, but finally took a few tentative steps forward. Her curiosity got the better of her, and she pressed her nose against the fence of Sasha's pen. Quick as lightning, Sasha patted Tibet on the nose.

"People ask me why I call Sasha a hooligan. That's a hooligan behavior if I've ever seen one. She didn't want to hurt Tibet—there was nothing malicious in it—but she deliberately gave her a pat on the nose. She wasn't trying to prove she was the boss or that she was strong—she just wanted to play."

Each day for several days, Earl led Tibet up to Sasha's cage. After a while, Tibet learned not to be afraid. Eventually, Earl put Sasha on a leash and walked around holding Sasha's leash in one hand and Tibet's lead rope in the other. Sasha enjoyed having additional company on the walks, and soon Tibet was trotting nonchalantly by her side. However, old Tibet stood less than thirty-one inches high. The point of the commercials was to have Earl look like a hero. Now that he had conditioned Sasha to accept the companionship of a horse, he had to find two horses who would accept her.

"I had more than a half dozen horses who had placid personalities, and I thought they would work well with a bear. But every time I'd try to introduce them to Sasha she would stand on her hind feet, making herself a very big bear. After seeing that, the horses refused to go near her. If I tried to force them, they would start head tossing, crow hopping, and dancing away. Keeping their eyes peeled on Sasha, they would get no closer than twenty-five feet."

Finally, Earl decided to concentrate on Best, a pony who had been in the family for years. She was as shrewd as an old fox and one of the most surefooted animals Earl had ever known. "You can race her at full gallop across a cornfield and never have to worry about tripping. She's a nice sized pony, and I wouldn't look too ridiculous on top of her for the commercials."

Like the other horses, however, Best insisted on keeping a certain distance between herself and Sasha. Earl needed help, and he recruited Sue Burroughs, a friend from New Jersey who was a superb horse-woman. Sue mounted Best, and Earl brought Sasha out of her pen on a leash and took her into the middle of a large horse ring. "As a rider, it was one of the most extraordinary experiences I've ever had," said Sue. "Sasha was very well behaved, but Best was terrified. I could sense it in every movement she made. She would not let that bear out of her sight, and consequently, she forgot to look where she was going. It took all my concentration not to fall off because she kept tripping. A ditch ran around the outer perimeter of the ring, and Best kept falling into it. We worked in the ring for a half hour, and then gave Best an hour break and brought her back into the ring. By the end of two days, her trembling had eased off. She was still wary, but she was no longer terrified. Then, every once in a while, Sasha would stand up on her hind legs, and that really freaked Best out. It freaked me out, too. I could catch sight of Sasha out of the corner of my eye, and I just wanted to split.

"I have ridden in championship horse shows, but I've never experienced anything so tense. I had to keep one eye on my horse, one eye on that darned bear, and I needed a third eye to watch the grinning creep in the middle who kept teasing me about coming in closer."

Eventually, Earl added Pinto, another horse, to the training ring. Seeing that Best was not terrified, Pinto adjusted much more quickly to the presence of a bear than Best had. After a week, the two horses were willing to go into the ring with Sasha in the middle, but they still insisted on a "flight" distance of about twenty feet.

"I was running out of time," says Earl. "I needed to find a way to condition the horses to a shorter flight distance. I decided to put them into the trailer and then put Sasha in the trailer in her cage. At first I only kept them in the trailer together for an hour or so, but I kept increasing the time until I kept them together all night. I knew that close confinement with Sasha would reassure the horses. She was unable to bother them because she was in her cage, and they became accustomed to her scent."

Earl planned on driving the animals to Minnesota. In order to cross state lines he needed various health certificates. He and Liz had only been in Tioga for a couple of months, and Dr. Farrell, the local veterinarian, was not yet used to their retinue of exotic animals. Earl drove over to his office with the horses and Sasha in the trailer.

"That's a very healthy-looking bear you've got there," Doctor Farrell commented, as the color drained from his face.

"Doc, don't you think you should take his temperature?" Earl asked.

"Oh, he looks very healthy to me." After his initial shocked reaction, Farrell gave Sasha a very professional examination. (He didn't have to take her temperature.) He signed the health certificates and wished them all a good time.

Earl hired two local boys to come along as assistants and they shared the driving chores. It was a long trip, but Earl found it incredibly beautiful. "The leaves were just beginning to turn. There were not many maples so the trees didn't turn a fiery red, but most were a beautiful golden yellow and there were lots of conifers, Norway and jack pine, and beautiful birch trees."

The commercials were to be filmed along a series of linked lakes surrounded by deep ragged rocky pine-covered trails. It was the North American watershed, sending waters north to the Hudson Bay, east to the Atlantic, and south to the Gulf of Mexico. This time there would be no difficulty in finding locations to symbolize "the land of sky-blue waters."

In order to house the production crew and the executives, the advertising agency had rented the entire Chik-Wawk Lodge on Saganaga Lake owned by Ralph and Bea Griffen. The California commercials had been on television in Minnesota for three months, and Earl had become something of a hero. Bea in particular was very excited to meet the rugged Hamm's man.

When Earl arrived, he felt very grubby from the long ride. The lake looked so cool and inviting he didn't even bother to take off his clothes. He tore off his boots and jumped in. "I almost had a heart attack, the water was so damn cold. I crawled out. Bea came running out to meet the rugged man from the commercials, and there I was, shivering like a damn fool, frozen stiff."

When Earl got up in the morning to check Sasha, he discovered bear tracks leading to and from the trailer. For a moment, he was terrified. Could Sasha have gotten loose? Then he heard her familiar thumping from inside in the trailer. Ralph was up early and explained to Earl that all the black bears in the area were in the habit of picking through the garbage from the lodge which was stored in a truck near the area where Earl had parked his trailer.

Earl quickly opened the trailer and led Best and Pinto out. "Those poor horses were in a state of panic. It was one thing to have gotten used to one bear, but they must have felt as if they had landed in the middle of bear city. They were so nervous I could hardly lead them down the road, much less work with them near Sasha.

"I told Rod and Lear they would have to call off any filming of the horses for the day. They were much too skittish to be worked." Earl checked on the horses periodically all day. By dusk, he decided to keep the horses up all night so that they would be tired for the filming. "I didn't want to use a tranquilizer on them. I don't like to use tranquilizers on general principle because I don't believe you should interfere with an animal's nervous—or muscular—system. Furthermore, the horses would need all their reflexes in case there was an emergency. I felt that if we just kept them walking slowly all night, they would be tired but still alert." From nine o'clock at night until eight in the morning, Earl and his helpers took turns walking the horses. At dawn, the horses were in fine shape, but Earl was exhausted.

After breakfast, Rod and Lear showed Earl the location they had chosen for the horses and Sasha. It was a gravel highway on top of a beautiful white bluff. There was a twenty-five-foot drop over the edge of the road, and Earl knew that if the horses panicked they might all go over the side. Yet it was incredibly beautiful, and Earl told them he would try it.

He went back to the trailer and got Sasha out of her cage. The air was cool. Earl had fed her only half the usual dinner the night before, and she was hungry and frisky, exactly the way he wanted her. His hope was that Sasha would go to the food and ignore the horses.

Lear set his cameras up. One of Earl's assistants

went up the road out of sight of the cameras, carrying Sasha's feed pan and a big stick. Earl had decided to stop feeding Sasha from the pouch he carried and had trained her to go from point A to point B at the sound of the rattle of her feed pan. This gave him a great deal of flexibility in directing her movements.

Earl's other assistants held the two horses while Earl held Sasha on her leash. Earl had arranged with Lear that he would not mount until Sasha heard the sound of her feed pan and started down the road. Then he would have Best and Pinto follow Sasha at a discreet distance. On film it would look as if they were on a pack trip together, but Earl hoped Sasha would be so intent on eating that she would not take too much notice of the horses behind her.

The first take went perfectly. Sasha rushed to her feed pan without turning around. Best and Pinto followed at a brisk trot. As long as the bear was ahead of them with her tiny remnant of a tail twitching, they were not nervous.

The crew wanted one more take. It took them about half an hour to rearrange the cameras for a different angle. During that time, Sasha grew bored and impatient. The edge of her hunger had been appeased by the apples in her feed pan.

When the cameramen yelled "Action!" Earl's assistant rattled the feed pan and Earl snapped off Sasha's leash and jumped on Pinto. At first, Sasha trotted down the road, her ears flicking back and forth at the sound of her feed pan. Halfway there, she wheeled around on her hind legs and suddenly faced the horses.

"She had a look in her eye. It was the fastest I've ever gotten off a horse. I jumped in front of the two horses and planted my feet wide apart, yelling, 'No, Sasha.' She was ready to have some fun with me. It was a real confrontation. Something had made her really test me in this situation. I bluffed her out. At the sound of my voice, she wheeled around and took off for her feed pan. They got a beautiful shot of her running toward the camera."

That night, Earl called Liz and told her what had happened. She was appalled. "Film crews have no idea of how dangerous it can be for Earl as well as for them. Can you imagine being the only person able to control a bear and two horses? You've only got two hands, two feet, and one head, after all. We had had such a hard time with the horses back in Tioga that I was afraid for Earl. I was frightened that he'd be watching the horses so much that he wouldn't be able to keep his eye on the bear."

Over the next few days the relationship between Earl and the film crew deteriorated. Three times he was told they would use the horses the next day. Each night, he and his assistants walked the horses up and down the road. In the morning Earl would discover that plans had been changed. When they did use the horses, Earl was tense.

In fairness to the agency and the production crew, the idea of using the horses and Sasha was Earl's in the first place; they would not have suggested it if he hadn't said it was possible. Furthermore, according to many, it was Earl who insisted on making the shots even more challenging. "I didn't want it to look too easy," he admits.

In fact, for all his complaining, it was Earl who came up with the idea that almost got him in serious trouble. He suggested that they film him forging a roaring river on horseback with Sasha at his side. Occasionally, even the most well-mannered horse will shy or balk at crossing a river, and the river Rod had chosen cascaded through deep woods. Huge black boulders provided a sharp contrast to the roaring white water. The rapids were so strong that Sasha took one look at them and decided this was one river she did not want to play in. Earl was mounted on Pinto, who was prancing by the river's side. Earl yelled at Sasha to get in the water. Because she usually bounded into rivers with great joy, Earl had not anticipated that this part would be a problem.

Sasha splashed in the water by the edge of the river, but kept her back legs firmly on the bank. Earl jumped off Pinto and handed the reins to his assistant. Pulling on Sasha's leash, he tried to force her into the water. "Daddy's getting pissed," he warned through gritted teeth.

"I have a temper I can't give away," admits Earl. As if she sensed Earl's tension, suddenly Sasha gave up her struggle and lumbered out into the middle of the river. She gave Earl a rueful look as if to say, "Okay, relax." Like a married couple with an unwritten contract, they have never both lost their tempers at the same time. They both seemed to sense that such an event would be fatal to one or the other.

"Sasha really helped me out at that moment. I don't like to romanticize our relationship. We're different species, and I can't possibly understand her motivations. I know she looks to me to feed her, and that is the bedrock of our relationship, but there are moments when it is deeper than that. I can't deny it.

So many women take offense because I call Sasha *she*. It's not because I think women are inferior. Liz and I are equal partners in our business. In fact, Liz keeps track of most of the business and is the president. Yet because we are man and wife, our relationship is more than a partnership. I think there are moments when the same holds true for me and Sasha, but on a different plane. We're partners because we work together. Yet sometimes there's an understanding between us that's akin to the feelings between two very close people."

Leaving Sasha in the middle of the river, Earl quickly went back for Pinto, who was reluctant to enter the river. Without wasting time, Earl grabbed her reins and led her into the river on foot.

There was no sand at the bottom of the river, and the space between the rocks was deep holes, made slippery by the constant pressure of the water.

"Sasha kept looking at me as if I had gone completely crazy, and I think she was right. The water was freezing. My legs were caught between boulders. We were lucky that none of us broke a leg."

Viewing the scene through his camera, Lear became excited. He realized it was one of the most beautiful shots he had filmed. "Can we get it one more time from a different angle?" he asked.

"Not on your life," shouted Earl. "Just get us out of here." An assistant took Pinto's reins, and Earl and Sasha picked their way to the shore. Sasha shook the water out of her fur. She looked up at Earl, and he says her eyes were twinkling. "Oh, she was laughing at me. The one good thing about my temper is that it goes quickly. Now that we were out of the river,

I thanked God they didn't use an actor for those scenes. Even when I'm mad, I still can gauge what we can and can't do. When they said, 'Let's try it one more time,' I said, 'Hell, no.' "

Luckily for Earl and Sasha, and for the crew that had to work with them, Ralph and Bea's lodge offered many opportunities for relaxation. Earl stayed by himself most of the time. He would wake up around 5:30 in the morning, when all the advertising and production people were still asleep, and in the early morning fog take Sasha out of her cage and walk her down to the edge of the lake.

A group of mallard ducks swam near the dock. They were practically tame because Ralph and Bea fed them, and each year they returned to the lake, staying until the water started to freeze. Even though it was now mid-October, and thousands of mallards had begun their migration, these ducks stayed.

At first, the ducks were frightened of Sasha; when she swam out to them, they quickly flew away. But soon they were alighting within ten feet of Sasha. Every day they narrowed the distance between them, until by the end of the week they would allow Sasha within a couple of feet.

"God, did Sasha love playing with those ducks," recalls Earl. "It's impossible to know whether strange friendships between species happen in the wild. I am sure that one of the reasons the ducks would play with Sasha was that they sensed that she was somehow different from wild bears. And, of course, they were tame. They would eat out of Ralph's or Bea's hand, and they had been returning to that lake for years.

Perhaps they sensed they had something in common with Sasha. Whatever it was, it was a delight to watch them together."

Once the filming with the horses was finished, Earl began to relax and enjoy himself. Lear had discovered a waterfall sixteen miles away that was accessible only by boat. It was spectacular, and Lear wanted a shot of Earl and Sasha standing next to it. Earl put Sasha in her transfer cage, and loaded her onto a speedboat. The waterfall was in Canada, and they had to go through customs. The officials laconically treated the flotilla of moviemakers and bear as if it were an everyday occurrence.

The filming at the waterfall went perfectly. Coming back, Earl decided to let Sasha out of her cage. Sasha rode in the bow, loving the feel of the wind on her fur.

"Twice she jumped out of the boat. The first time, she turned around and gave me a 'watch-me' look and all of a sudden she was off and into the water. We cut the motor quickly so she wouldn't be hurt. We couldn't haul her into the boat again, because she would have capsized us in a second, so we had to head to the shore of the nearest island.

"The second time it was an accident. She was bouncing around next to me and we hit the wake of another boat. She just bounced out of the boat. I saw the expression on her face when she hit the water and she was shocked. We got her to an island again, but she didn't want to come back into the boat. She thought the boat had just pushed her in. Finally, after a great deal of waiting on my part and consumption of marshmallows in Sasha's part, Sasha agreed to get back in the boat. She got in and we made it home."

After observing how comfortable Sasha was in a boat, the client asked Earl if he could put Sasha in a canoe. They wanted some still photographs of Earl and Sasha in a canoe on the "sky-blue waters."

Over fifty years ago, the very first advertisements for Hamm's Beer had been photographed in this area of Minnesota. One of the owners of Hamm's Beer was an outdoorsman who spent each summer fishing on Saganaga Lake. According to the stories told today, those first photographic sessions were extraordinarily casual and spontaneous. The owner forgot to bring up a camera. He also forgot to bring along some of his own beer. He had to borrow a camera from one of the local guides, and he and his friends rummaged through the dump until they found six Hamm's beer bottles that they cleaned up and put in a six-pack.

In 1973, the budget for the commercials was well over $100,000, and 15 cases of beer were on hand. Dozens upon dozens of beer cans would be used to film one perfect bottle opening.

Instead of forgetting their camera, the agency had arranged for Les Blacklock, the celebrated nature photographer, to come and take still photographs of Earl and Sasha.

Earl was fascinated by Blacklock's approach to nature. "He's one of the finest outdoorsmen I've ever met, but he's completely different from what I imagined an outdoorsman to be and he taught me a lot.

I think of myself as an outdoorsman, but I am always so busy either farming or fishing or working with animals that I don't take the time to look closely. When he's walking in the woods, Les will bend down and study one leaf for a long time and with great pleasure. The man could live in the woods for six months, not travel over a hundred feet in any direction, and never be bored. And he still wouldn't see everything he wanted to see. Les has the sensitivity to capture what everybody else has missed."

Ralph and Bea had an old eighteen-foot freighter canoe that they had restored and fitted with a little ten horsepower motor. Ralph volunteered its use for Les Blacklock's photograph of Earl and Sasha.

Earl took Sasha down to the dock, and Les and Ralph slipped the canoe alongside. Sasha stepped into the canoe very willingly. Only a few days before she had enjoyed her ride in the flat-bottomed motorboat. However, as soon as she put her weight into the canoe, it started to bob and she struggled to get out of the canoe, and Earl helped her back onto the dock. "I didn't want to make the canoe a battle. She and I had been having enough hard times. I tied her to a tree near the edge of the lake, and Ralph and I tried to figure out if there was anything we could do to make the canoe stable. Ralph is the kind of person who enjoys having a problem to solve."

Ralph brought his front-end loader down to the beach and dug up a pile of sand. They put nearly 300 pounds of sand into the bottom of the canoe for ballast. The three men stood on the gunwales, and with their combined weight, the canoe sank deeper into the water until it rested a few inches above the surface. When they jumped up and down in it, the canoe barely shifted.

Earl untied Sasha and brought her back to the dock. She was in a good mood and once again willingly climbed into the canoe. Les and Ralph pushed them off and Earl started the engine. Sasha started to bounce around: When the canoe didn't rock, she began to enjoy herself. Les got some beautiful pictures of her hanging over the bow, her huge paws dangling in the water.

After Les said he had enough pictures, Earl decided to take Sasha out for a canoe ride just for fun. When they were in the middle of the lake, Sasha decided it would be more fun to ride in the back with Earl. She managed to turn herself around in the bow and headed for the stern. The ballast was weighted for Sasha in the front. If she came back, Earl knew they would soon be shipping water.

He yelled, "No, Sasha!"

"She gave me a strange look as if to say, 'Why not?' She was in a marvelous mood," recalls Earl. "She just thought it would be fun to sit next to me. Finally, she seemed to understand that she had to stay in the front and she returned to the bow, but she still found a way to get into trouble. She leaned way out over the water, dipping her paw in and creating a draw, and so she shipped water her way."

Sasha then pulled her paw out of the water and placed her two front paws on the gunwales, raising her nose to the wind. Lear and Rod came to the edge of the lake and decided to film it. One of the most beautiful scenes in all the commercials is of Earl and Sasha in the canoe in the early morning fog. They pull into a campsite, and once they've settled, Earl snaps off the pop tab of a can of beer.

Earl was in the habit of putting the ring tab in his beer or soda can before he took his first sip. "I don't like to leave any litter," he says. "It's easy to flip those tops, put the ring down, and forget about it. If you get into the habit of slipping it into the drink, it becomes second nature. I did it on camera and Lear filmed it. Rod wanted me to do it because he's an outdoorsman, as concerned about litter as I am. In fact, it might have been Rod's idea."

When the commercial was shown on the air, Rod and Earl were surprised at the amount of mail they received objecting. People wrote that it was unsanitary and dangerous. Apparently, the ring can come out of the can and choke the person drinking it. Earl had difficulty taking the complaints seriously. "I bet someone's cousin by their late uncle on the wife's side of the family—a damn idiot—choked . . . and he knew he put it there."

Rod wasn't upset by the complaining letters. "It proved that people watched the commercials so closely that they caught that small gesture. Most of the letters began, 'We love your commercials, but. . . .' I'm happy to generate that kind of controversy." In the next series of commercials shot several months later, Rod rectified matters. His storyboards called for Earl to pull off a ring tab and put the tab in his pocket.

During the last days of filming in Minnesota, Earl and Sasha spent every spare moment in the canoe.

"I don't think the two of us have ever done anything together that was as much fun. As soon as work was over, I'd slip away with Sasha in our canoe. We'd explore the entire area. Everyone was afraid we'd get lost. All the lakes are connected and look pretty much the same, and there are islands upon islands. We'd travel miles, going about 8 mph. People would be fishing, and most of them would do a double take when they saw a bear, but some would just look up and go right back to their fishing. I guess those were the *real* fishermen. One day we covered sixteen miles coming back to Ralph and Bea's by canoe.

"I was terribly impressed with the women up in the north woods. They were the hardy ones. You talk about men with the pioneer spirit, but I kept running into women who ran the post offices all by themselves, delivering mail by boat, and women who were competent fishing guides. They were interested in Sasha, and they would come alongside in their boats and ask me more intelligent questions than I get from most men who claim to be outdoorsmen.

"Sometimes we would hit rapids. I'd have to take them just right because there might be a foot's difference between the water level in one lake and another. The submerged rocks made it dangerous because we could have broken the motor easily, and I didn't relish the idea of trying to paddle back with 300 pounds of ballast and a 700-pound bear.

"As Sasha became more confident, she began to love the rapids. She would bounce around the bow, ready for mischief. A couple of times, she'd be carrying on so much that she'd fall overboard. She always acted shocked, as if her feelings were hurt. She'd swim for the closest island and then get back into the canoe. . . . Lordy, she and I had such wonderful times in that canoe."

When Earl was packing for the trip back to Tioga, Ralph came to his room to visit. He asked Earl if he wanted a large freighter canoe for his own.

"Would I want one?" asked Earl incredulously. "Are you kidding?"

"What would you give for one?" Ralph asked.

"My left arm."

"Why not your right arm?"

"I might need that one."

"I'll tell you what, Earl. There's been an eighteen-foot canoe lying around here for a few years, and if you and Sasha want it, it's yours."

"I consider that one of the greatest gifts I've ever received. I brought it back to Tioga, and Sasha and I use it on the large pond in back. Sasha will eventually have to be retired. She gets bigger and bigger, and the proportion between man and bear will no longer look right on camera. I can always look at the commercials if I want to remember some of the good times we've had, but the commercials don't mean anything to Sasha. Yet when she and I take that big canoe out on the pond in Tioga, I know Sasha will be recalling the great times we had.

"I'll never forget one of our last days out in Minnesota. Sasha and I were riding in the back of a pickup truck. We were both standing up, looking over the cab of the truck. Suddenly, out of nowhere, a moose popped out of the woods and trotted down the road after us.

"Sasha looked at me. I looked at Sasha.

"I said, 'What the hell, Sasha! You're in a pickup truck with me . . . why shouldn't there be a moose on the road?'

"She looked at me, and I felt she was suddenly asking herself, '*What am* I doing in a pickup truck with a *man*?'

"Then, I swear to God, she laughed."

Mignon and Leonard romping in pastures
of farm in Tioga, Pennsylvania.

41   Mignon gets her bottle from Niki in kitchen.

Mignon gets her bottle from Jenny
while Priscilla Llama watches.

43   Mignon gets her bottle from a very pregnant Liz.

Mignon practices her small repertoire of tricks.   (*Right*)   44

Mignon and Leonard share a drink.

Mignon learns to give Niki a ride.　　　**46**

47 Mignon needs all the help she can get. She uses Liz's stomach for support while Jenny, Missy Westbrook, and Dog push.

49   Mignon overturning her food bucket.

50   Mignon and Dandelion, on a stroll,
run into Luke, their black bear cub.

Niki and Munchie Wolf.   51

Jenny and Luke play hide-and-seek.

Jenny lets Priscilla Llama sniff her flower.   **53**

54   Liz and Mignon exchange kisses.

11

Adjusting to Farm Life

While Earl was in Minnesota, Liz, Niki, Jenny, and Mignon began their adjustment to farm life. Mignon became accustomed to her new home quickly, and the sight of her emerging from the basement into the kitchen soon became the talk of the neighborhood.

There was no direct route from the basement to outside, and in order to take her daily walk, Mignon had to be led up the cellar steps and through the kitchen. It was an arrangement that suited Mignon perfectly. On her way out, she could snatch a stray piece of toast or a piece of candy.

"Because she walked through the kitchen every day, I still felt she was part of the family. It was a very nice, homey feeling. She would take drinks out of the sink the way she used to in Jersey," says Liz.

Liz combined her daily walk with Mignon with trips to the pastures to check on the cows. The previous owner's herd of forty Hereford did not exactly know what to make of Mignon. The first time she and Liz ambled into their pasture, they stared at Mignon, turned tail, and ran. As soon as Mignon saw they were more frightened than she was, she gained courage and ran after them, her trunk straight out. As they ran further into their pastures, the cows turned to take another look at the strange new creature. At about a hundred feet from them, Mignon stopped, gave a cry of alarm, and came running back to Liz.

"Mignon was changing. She was much more adventurous than she had been at Volney's. She reminded me of Niki and Jenny when they were toddlers. One moment she would want to explore on her own, the next moment she'd be running back for Mommy. Both Niki and Jenny used to have periods when they played as if they hardly knew me, then, seconds later, they'd come flying back to my arms or tug on my knees. Then they'd be off again.

"Mignon couldn't tug at my knees. She was already almost as tall as I was, but she would do the equivalent. She would cling to me with her trunk, and then she'd run off again."

Within a week, Mignon and the cows had worked up a routine. Liz believes the cows were only trying to keep a distance, but Mignon was playing a game. "She would go running up to them and wave her trunk to scare them away, then she would come running back to me. She loved it. If the cows weren't around, she would go looking for them. She learned all their favorite places to rest, their secret gullies. She even learned their daily routines. She would know in the morning that they might be down near the beaver pond, while in the afternoons they preferred the shade of the woods."

When Earl returned from Minnesota, he bought a young registered bull. The old bull had been part of the herd for many years, and the herd had a few generations of inbred stock. Earl hoped the new bull would upgrade the herd. The bull had a red circle around his eye which naturally led to the name Red-Eye, and he took command of the herd with authority. Red-Eye had been conditioned to believe that anything large with four legs had been put into the pasture for his pleasure, and Liz did not like the way he looked at Mignon. She suspected that he might try to mount her.

Even if he resisted that temptation, Liz was afraid he would think Mignon was a challenger. "She was so goofy, squealing and running back and forth, he just didn't know what to make of her. He stood his ground in front of his herd, and I believe Mignon sensed that he wasn't like the other cows and that he wouldn't tolerate her antics. If she had been part of an elephant herd, she would have learned which elephants like to play and which ones have a quick temper. I think she understood Red-Eye's vibrations, and she tried to avoid him."

Gradually, Red-Eye cut down Mignon's playtime with his herd. Luckily, by then Mignon had discovered another companion, Priscilla the llama.

Liz had bought Priscilla because she loved llamas and they let her roam the pastures at will. She stayed apart from the cows, and Liz loved watching her out in the fields. Llamas are members of the camel family, and when Priscilla ran across the pastures, it was easy to understand why camels are called ships of the desert.

"When Earl and I went to the Catskill game farm to pick out Priscilla," says Liz, "we had over sixty baby llamas to choose from. I made my choice while Earl was looking at some other animals. Then I went off to look at the zebras, and Earl looked over the llamas. We hadn't talked to each other. He didn't know which llama I had picked, yet we both chose Priscilla."

As the air became cooler, and the trees lost their leaves, Liz, Priscilla, and Mignon explored the boundaries of their property. Usually Liz waited until Niki and Jenny came home from school, and they would all go on a walk.

Liz had learned she was pregnant and the baby was due in the spring. Just as Mignon was becoming more determined in her explorations, Liz's pregnancy slowed her down. She needed Niki to take Mignon for walks. "Niki really played the older sister as she would have if they had been sisters in a herd. In the herd, when the mother gives birth to a baby, the older sister or other members of the herd take on much of the responsibility for the younger elephants. They run after them and keep them out of trouble. Niki couldn't run as fast as Mignon, and that was unfortunate, but Mignon would (at least occasionally) listen to her, and she definitely was a help in keeping her under control."

One of their greatest problems was that Mignon was huge for an elephant her age. She was not fat, because she got so much exercise, but she was practically twice the size of most Indian elephants her age. Earl attributed her size to the high vitamin content of her meals. All of the Hammonds' exotic animals—Donna Rae, Sasha, Moose, and Mignon—get fresh vegetables, not just as a special treat, but as part of their regular diet. Earl and Liz feel strongly that their animals will remain healthier if they eat a variety of foods. They don't believe that vitamin supplements are a substitute for the natural vitamins in fresh foods.

Liz's trip to the supermarket had a certain silent comedy flavor at that time. Liz, Niki, and Jenny would each take a cart and go directly to the fruit and vegetable section to see what was on sale. They grabbed up overripe bananas as fast as the man could mark them down. The owners learned to bring out all their slightly spoiled vegetables whenever the Hammonds came in. On one typical trip, Liz bought thirty-four bunches of bananas, twenty-eight family-sized loaves of bread, eighteen pounds of apples, two cartons of evaporated milk (Mignon continued to get her bottles), three bags of onions—one of Mignon's favorite vegetables—and a couple of pork roasts for the human family.

One day a woman patiently stood behind them while the clerk rang up their bill: $90.90. The woman held a package of Certs in her hand. While Liz wrote out a check, the woman asked in a quiet voice, "Excuse me, is this ten cents?"

"Good Lord," exclaimed Liz. "Why didn't you ask to go ahead of me? You didn't have to wait just for that."

The woman shook her head. "I had to watch it. I couldn't believe one person was buying all that."

The woman never asked her why she was buying such a huge and curious selection of groceries. "I always expected people to ask whether we ran an orphanage or what. But I rarely got questioned. A few people would stare at us, but they almost never spoke to us. It was very peculiar."

In early December, Volney drove up for his first visit to the farm. Liz made an elaborate oyster chowder, and they stayed up talking late into the night. In the morning, everyone piled into the truck and gave Volney a complete tour of the farm, showing him the beaver ponds and the woods, inspecting all the cattle. The size of the place worried Volney. He thought the farm needed too much work, and it would cause them many headaches. Yet he seemed to understand how much it meant to Liz and Earl to have a place of their own.

Liz and Earl felt a great satisfaction at having Volney as *their* guest. At night they showed Volney the commercials Earl had made, and in the morning when he left, they loaded his truck with twenty bales of hay, several chickens, and some wild boar meat.

Shortly after Volney left, a young couple barely out of their teens, Ed and Missy Westbrook, stopped at the farm. They had lived in New Jersey near Volney's and they were on their way to the northwest. They were only going to stay a couple of hours, but Liz and Earl convinced them to spend the night. The next morning, Missy and Ed helped with the chores, and in midafternoon Liz and Earl took them for a walk accompanied by Niki, Jenny, Mignon, and Dog. The temperature had fallen to 15°. There was snow on the ground, and Niki and Jenny made snowballs and threw them at Mignon.

"You can't let your sisters get away with that,"

admonished Liz. She made a snowball and placed it in the tip of Mignon's trunk. "You can learn to throw a snowball," she said. As she spoke, Liz guided Mignon's trunk up and helped her send the snowball sailing.

"Try it yourself," suggested Liz, handing her a second snowball. Mignon lifted her trunk and the snowball wavered in the air and landed at her feet. Niki threw one and hit Mignon broadside. Liz handed Mignon another snowball. This time the snowball lofted into the air and landed two feet in front of Niki. Everyone applauded. Using her front foot and trunk to gather the snow together, Mignon made her own snowball, raised her trunk, and let it fly. Niki ran toward it, letting it hit her on the shoulder. Mignon did a little dance of excitement as everyone applauded.

Continuing their walk through the woods, Mignon constantly carried a snowball in her trunk. When they approached the beaver pond, she broke away from the group and skittered out onto the ice.

"She had a new trick that only I had seen, and she wanted to show off," explains Liz. "It started the first time ice formed on the back pasture. She loved the sensation of her feet sliding out from under. It didn't frighten her at all—she would try to make her feet go faster and faster until it looked as if she were doing a dance."

When Earl saw Mignon sliding on the ice, he yelled at her to get back on solid ground, but she ignored him and continued her Charleston. Earl was afraid Mignon might break a leg, but Liz felt Mignon was so relaxed that even if she fell she wouldn't hurt herself. Liz walked ahead with Missy because she wanted to show her a particularly beautiful spot up on a hill. Earl decided to go out on the ice after Mignon.

Liz heard Earl yell, "No! Mignon!" She turned around to see Earl slipping on the ice himself, pushing Mignon to the edge of the pond. Forced off her ice, Mignon charged up the hill toward Liz with her trunk straight out, making high-pitched shrieks as she ran. "It was so funny. I knew she was saying, 'Mommy, tell Daddy I'm allowed to ice-skate.' She hid behind me. Even six months pregnant, I could not hide an elephant. Earl came panting up the hill, so mad at her, but when he saw her hiding behind me, he just cracked up."

As they walked back to the house, Earl spotted a red-tailed hawk circling over the farmland they now owned. He pointed it out to the others. "There's so much to be done with birds of prey. So many eagles and falcons and hawks are stagnating in zoos and so many get shot by hunters and nobody has the time to teach them how to fly again. Someday, I'd like to open a center for breeding endangered species and work with birds of prey. I hope the profits from the wildlife adventure movie I want to make will give me enough money to do some work with threatened species."

That night Liz cooked chicken laced with apple brandy, and Ed brought out his guitar and sang some songs he had written, struggling to raise his voice over Mignon's occasional trumpets from the basement.

In the morning, Missy and Ed decided to stay awhile longer, and ended up staying for over two years. Missy and Ed's arrival on the heels of Volney's visit completed a cycle. When Liz had moved into Volney's, she had been about Missy's age. Now she and Earl had a home of their own, and she would teach others about animals the way she had learned from Volney and Lorrain.

One terrible winter day, there was an ice storm. Liz and Missy took Mignon out for a few minutes and came scurrying back, trying to protect their faces from the ice pellets. Liz rubbed Mignon down with a blanket, and suddenly she realized that it had been days since she had seen Priscilla. Later that night Liz mentioned to Earl that she was worried about Priscilla in the ice storm, but Earl told her she was being overly anxious. Llamas are perfectly acclimatized to winter. In Peru they survive in the harsh climate of the Andes, and they are among the world's most surefooted animals. Though they are commonly believed to be cloven-hooved, they actually have two toes and can move in icy and mountainous terrain with great agility.

Liz assumed Priscilla was off in the woods somewhere and stopped worrying. But the next day while Earl was in the tractor feeding the cattle, he tried to find Priscilla and couldn't. Now it was his turn to worry. "I knew it was irrational and unrealistic to worry about her, but somehow I felt she was in trouble."

Earl began to comb the property for her, although looking for a white llama in an ice storm is not easy. Finally, he came upon her. She was lying on the ground barely able to lift her head. Her eyes had begun to glaze over. He picked her up and cradled her in his arms, her long neck slung over his shoulder.

When he got back to the house, he laid her down on the floor in the kitchen near the stove. Jenny and Niki grabbed blankets off their beds and covered her while Earl forced liquor down her throat. Sometimes liquor will act as a stimulant, but Earl was not hopeful. "It's funny about llamas. They don't have much fight in them. They are such hardy animals, but when they go, they won't fight for their lives the way some animals will." Priscilla began making grunting noises deep in her throat as if her lungs were congested.

Dr. Farrell came and examined her, but agreed with Earl that she was close to death. "We hate to give up on an animal," said Liz. Farrell injected her with large doses of antibiotics and electrolytes, but Priscilla died about twenty minutes later.

Both Earl and Liz react with anger to the death of one of their animals, but for slightly different reasons.

"I get mad," says Earl, "because we give our animals such a tremendous amount of care, and then I feel so helpless."

Liz gets upset because it always seems to her that they lose the good ones. "Your scruffs never die. Priscilla was such a sweetheart of a llama. Your real winners just go *pffttt*, and your dimwits live forever. It's heartbreaking."

The next morning Earl put Priscilla in the back of the Land-Rover, and he and Liz drove to the vet's. "I always want to know what killed one of my animals so I can try to keep it from happening again," says Earl. Dr. Farrell discovered that Priscilla died of infectious bovine rhinotracheatus, a highly infectious disease. Liz and Earl were afraid it would spread to their other animals. They realized they would have to test and inoculate all their cattle, goats, and Moose. Fortunately, the disease could not affect Mignon nor any of the horses.

Vaccination day began calmly enough. The ice storm had abated, but it had gotten colder, making the ground icy and footing treacherous. Liz's plaid jacket barely zipped over her bulging belly, and Earl held her hand as they tried to maneuver themselves up the hill toward Moose's pen. They had decided to inoculate him first.

Liz lured Moose over to the fence with an apple, and when his velvet muzzle was pressed against the chain links, Earl squirted vaccine into it, saying, "Sorry, big boy, I know this is going to make you mad, but it's better than getting sick." Moose shook his head violently. "It's going to be all right," crooned Earl, handing Moose apples and chocolate chip cookies.

After inoculating the goats and sheep, it was time to vaccinate the cows.

Earl mounted his horse to start the roundup. The weather had turned cooler; it was now 8° and the wind was rising. The cattle had to be driven through the gate of the upper pasture, down past the road in front of the house, and into the barn.

When all the cattle had been herded into the barn, the noise was deafening. The cows bellowed and defecated as cows do in a clean barn.

In order to be vaccinated, each cow would have to be maneuvered so that its head was between the metal bars of the stanchions. The traditional method for getting a cow to put its head through the stanchion is to put sweet grain in front of the bars. The cow has to reach its head through the bars to get at the grain.

Unfortunately, the cattle were so excited and nervous they showed little interest in the sweet grain. Missy and Ed could not seem to do anything right. Every time they moved, they would inevitably startle a cow just when Earl or Liz had it near the stanchions. Even after Earl had successfully coaxed a cow between the bars, more often than not, the lever mechanism was rusted and the bars did not swing shut. The cow casually lifted its head out and rejoined the herd.

In pure frustration, Earl tried to herd one cow by grabbing it by the tail and pulling with all his might. The 1300-pound cow struggled to break free and easily did, huddling in a far corner in the middle of a group of cows. Grabbing a two-by-four, Earl thrust himself into the middle of the herd, cutting out the recalcitrant cow. When the cow tried to slip around him, Earl made a threatening half swing with the two-by-four, yelling at the top of his lungs, "THINK—GODDAMN IT!"

It was now late afternoon, and all had been up since early morning with nothing to eat since breakfast. Missy and Ed stood by the side covered in muck and cold.

"I don't want lunch," muttered Earl. "Get everybody out of here."

Liz, Ed, and Missy walked up the hill to the house. Lunch was eaten in exhausted silence. After about ten minutes, Liz went back down to the barn. Without saying a word, she and Earl calmly moved around the cows, cooing and crooning to them and luring them with sweet grain.

Forty-five minutes later, Missy and Ed walked back down to the barn. Earl was sitting back on his haunches smoking a cigarette. Every cow had its head through a stanchion and was placidly eating sweet grain. Earl had a smile of delighted triumph on his face.

"Now that I've had more experience with animals, I understand his frustration," says Ed. "You can't really teach someone to make the right moves around animals; they have to learn it by osmosis. Earl gets furious when he thinks someone might hurt themselves because they don't know what they're doing. When we were gone, Earl was able to handle all the cows himself."

Working quietly, Liz, Earl, Ed, and Missy quickly vaccinated all the cows and let them back out to pasture. Later that night, while Ed strummed his guitar, Earl helped Liz practice her natural childbirth exercises. The baby was due in less than a month.

12

Sasha and People

While Earl was slipping and sloshing in the muck, his image continued to flash across the screen wherever Hamm's was sold. In survey after survey, the commercials were rated over every other brand of beer in visual interest and popularity.

Hamm's was sold to the Olympia Beer Company, and although the new owners were glad to acquire a product for which there was such a strong positive consumer identification, they were not completely happy with the commercials. Their market surveys showed that Hamm's Beer appealed primarily to older people. Young people liked the commercials, but didn't buy the beer. They told researchers that Hamm's had an "old man's image"; it was the beer their fathers drank.

Even though Earl was only thirty-six when the commercials began, he presented the image of a loner, not a young man. Occasionally he would come out of the woods to stop in a tavern for a beer, but basically he was shown as a rugged individualist, and he came across as someone who really didn't need anybody else, except, of course, Sasha.

The Olympia marketing executives spoke to the executives at Dancer, Fitzgerald, and Sample about coming out with a campaign that would appeal to the eighteen-to-twenty-eight-year-old market. Rod Mac-Nicholl immediately came up with the idea of a series of commercials with an ecological theme. "Of course," says Rod, "much of the real work in ecology is done by hunters and fishermen—people in their forties, fifties, or sixties, but nevertheless, ecology has a youthful image. It's obviously Earl's type of thing, and it would be a way of getting him with young people."

Rod envisioned commercials in which young people would be doing something ecologically useful, such as planting trees after a forest fire. Earl and Sasha would walk into the middle of the scene, and the young people would greet them. Earl would help them plant, and then they would all have a beer together. The audience was to feel that young people trusted Earl and Sasha and would naturally want to drink a beer with them. Rod has always maintained that the commercials are a fantasy, and this would be taking the fantasy one step further. In reality, if any young people came upon a man and a bear in the wild, they would be wise to run for their lives.

Before going any further with these storyboards, Rod checked with Earl to find out if it was feasible for Sasha to work in close contact with so many strangers. One very good reason why Earl had been portrayed as a loner was that, in the filming of previous commercials, Earl had been the only one close enough to Sasha to get hurt. The film crew was always several feet away from Sasha. However, for the new commercials Sasha would have to work closely with half a dozen strangers. Although Earl was familiar with her behavior patterns and responses, she could behave unpredictably. On the other hand, Earl knew that she had enjoyed the filming of the other commercials. "She loves the variety of each day, and she loves attention. While it is true that bears in the wild are solitary creatures, Sasha has never been in the wild; she has a fairly sociable personality. She also has an incredible amount of curiosity, and she loves to have things going on around her. I don't want to imply that I understand her completely, or even that I trust her, but I do know her well enough to know that she is not vicious."

A bear's behavior is part instinct and part learned. In his book about Kodiaks, Roger Caras states: "It is probably true that since the bear is a higher animal, most of his instincts are open-ended, little more than a potential pattern of behavior or set of responses waiting to be influenced by what is learned. Since no two bears live the same life any more than two people do, no two bears are exactly the same. Each bear is a totally unique result of common instincts, uncommonly influenced by the accidents of existence."

Sasha's "accident of existence" had led her to experience rewards only from humans. All her food came from Earl. When she played, she played with Earl at her side. Bears in the wild learn to fear people because they carry guns, but Sasha had no reason to fear people. Earl knew that these commercials would be more difficult than the others because they would be using more people, but he felt that they could be made successfully *if* he were given time to teach the people how to act around her. He told Rod he would undertake the commercials only if the agency would allow four days of on-location training for everyone who would be used.

Rod told him he could have his four days and that he could replace or remove anyone who he felt did not have the right personality to work with Sasha. Earl told Rod to pick the extras and in the meantime, back at the farm, he began training Ed to assist him with Sasha.

The advertising agency gave Lear Levin and his associates the job of choosing the extras. They had to find fourteen attractive-looking young people who would look comfortable in the outdoors and who could be trusted to use common sense around the bear. Lear and his production assistant Lesley Mac-Neil pulled together an unusual crew; it included an Outward Bound instructor from Jackson Hole, Wyoming, an ex-Marine swimming pool salesman, a cartoonist who was from Maine, and two actors who worked in experimental theater in New York. Lear and Lesley felt that each one of them could be trusted not to panic.

"For this series, I think it helped that most of the extras were not actors," explained Lesley. "Too often the actor in a commercial is nervous because the success or failure of the commercial is so important to his or her career. But everyone here had another career. They came because they wanted some extra money and because they thought it would be interesting. So they were a fairly relaxed bunch."

The commercials were to be shot in northern Georgia, a spectacular area where the Chattahoochee River cuts its way through the Smokies. (Much of the film *Deliverance* was shot there.) The extras and the crew, twenty-six people in all, flew down, while Earl and Ed drove Sasha down in the trailer.

They arrived in the middle of the night. Abby Costello, one of the extras, recalls that she was asleep "when all of a sudden I began to hear a rhythmical clanging noise. I woke my husband, Tom, and said, 'Listen to that. What the hell do you think it is?' Then we realized it must be the bear. She was rocking her cage back and forth in the van.

"Suddenly we started to imagine the size of this animal—it sounded as if it were rocking the whole parking lot. The next morning, even before Earl was up, people from the town started to gather. They climbed on top of Sasha's van and peeked through the air vents. She started to roar, and I began to think about what I had gotten myself into."

The next day, Earl held a meeting with the entire crew. He said a few words about Sasha, making a special point of explaining that her claws had not been ripped out, her paws had not been broken, and that she was, in reality, a male and had not been castrated. The main thing he tried to impress upon them was that she might look as sweet and cuddly as a teddy bear, but that she was a potentially dangerous animal.

"Basically, if you do what I say, nothing will go wrong," Earl reassured them. "I can read Sasha's movements. I know what her moods are, what her feelings are, and what she is likely to do. The first few days that we work together, I'm going to be reading *your* bodies and *your* motions, not your words. We've got four days, and that will give me plenty of time to introduce you to Sasha and for her to get to know you. If you feel particularly anxious once we have begun to work with her, tell me. You and I can spend a little extra time with the bear."

Doug Coffin, the cartoonist, believes that the first night set the tone for the entire shooting. "The first reason I trusted Earl was that he handled us so well. He did not say, 'Some of you may make it, and some of you may not.' He said, 'I don't think there will be any trouble.' Then he laid down certain simple rules —that we should not make any sudden movements or sharp noises around Sasha. Basically, he made it clear that he wanted us to get along with the bear, and very evidently he wanted the bear to get along with us. It was obvious to us that he wanted the whole situation to work. I felt that he was a man who really knew what he was doing and who was tremendously patient and logical."

The next morning, Earl divided the entire crew into groups of four. He asked each group to stand in a wide semicircle and gave each person a pole to hold. He told them to hold the poles at the top with their fingers facing inward. Then he brought Sasha out on a leash. Earl walked with Sasha to each person in turn. As she sniffed them, Earl instructed the extras to stand quietly and keep the poles between themselves and Sasha. Sasha sniffed each pole, and then, as she usually did with Earl, she lifted her head to the extra's hands. "Curve your fingers in so she won't think they're nibbles," admonished Earl. Slowly Sasha licked each extra's hands.

"When I first met Sasha, I didn't realize how frightened I would be," admits Coffin. "I told myself I trusted Earl and that nothing bad would happen, but my hands were gripping the pole so tightly that my knuckles turned white. When Earl and Sasha came up to me, Earl asked me to lift the pole a couple of inches off the ground. I tried, but I couldn't.

"Earl said, 'It doesn't mean anything at all. You're just a little tense. Take a few steps back.' The next day, when Earl brought Sasha over to me, he alluded to my nervousness very openly, and consequently, I felt much more relaxed. I didn't feel like I had to hide my feelings."

When Sasha began to lick his hand, Coffin told Earl, "It feels fine, soft and strange, but my heart is racing."

Earl replied, "It should . . . that's good. As long as it doesn't show in your body, your heart can race away."

On the second day, Earl asked each person to take a walk beside him while Sasha was still on her leash. The procedure was very orderly, the way they had practiced it on the first day. Each person stood in place, holding a pole in front of his or her body. Earl and Sasha would walk up, and Earl would give Sasha a chance to sniff the person out, lick his or her pole, lick his or her hand. Then he would tell the person to begin walking, and he and Sasha would follow. "During those first two days, I concentrated on their faces and bodies," says Earl. "In a sense, Sasha was secondary. I had her on a leash, and I would only work her a few minutes and then give her a break. At some visceral level, I'm very conscious of Sasha at every moment, but I had to concentrate on the people and what their bodies were telling me. People can tell me, 'Oh, I'm not afraid of animals,' but nothing teaches me as much about their feelings toward animals as the way they hold their hands, the angles of their heads, the looks in their eyes, the way they stand and move.

"I wanted them to get used to Sasha licking their hands because it is the best way for them to get over their fear, and it is the best way for me to learn who is the most afraid. But while I wanted them to lose their initial fear, I did not want them to become foolhardy. I have to give Lear and Lesley tremendous credit for their choice of people. None of them tried to prove to me 'how good they were with animals.' Those are the kind of people who are likely to get your animal in trouble."

On the third day, Earl took Sasha off her leash and had the groups crisscross in front of her. Sasha was a little bit hungry, and Eddie stood about a hundred yards away, banging her feed pan with a stick. Sasha ignored the people walking near her and went directly to her feed pan.

All went smoothly until one moment when Abby Costello was a couple of feet in front of Sasha. Suddenly, Sasha roared. "She actually spoke English," recalls Tom Costello. "She said, 'Mmooooove.' It was an *m* sound and it was quite shocking. I was standing behind Sasha, looking at my wife. I felt a tremendous twitch down my leg. It was an impulse to jump, but I knew from everything Earl had told us that the worst thing I could do was to make a sudden move."

After her roar, Sasha stood with all four paws on the ground, but she had shifted her weight so her right front paw was loose. Earl quickly stepped in between Sasha and Abby. He waited a second, giving Sasha a chance to adjust to his change of position. Then he popped her on the nose. She blinked her eyes, and then walked quietly to her feed pan.

"I thought time had stopped," says Tom Costello. "I know only a second went by between the time Sasha roared and the time Earl stepped between them, but it felt as if everything, including my heart, had stopped."

At the end of their four training days, Earl gathered the group together. He said, "I feel you all know how to act. Now that we are about to start filming, I'm not going to be looking at you. You've learned what there is to learn. I'm going to be concentrating on Sasha. If anyone has a problem, tell me. I'm relying on your honesty. Basically, it's my job to watch Sasha, to watch her moods. I'm counting on you to react in the ways I've taught you. Always hold a pole in front of you. Walk slowly, but with assurance. If you are still afraid, come and talk to me and we will do some extra work."

The shooting of the commercials in Georgia was much more complex than the other ones Lear had made with Earl and Sasha. This time he could not simply collect as many beautiful seconds of footage as possible and then splice them together. Each of these new commercials had to tell a short story. According to Rod MacNicholl, as with anything complicated, there were so many things against its coming out well. "The clients were terrified of wasting their money. It cost $250,000 to $300,000 just for six 30-second commercials. That's astronomical. However, the likelihood was that we would end up with more than six commercials, because if they were successful, we could cut them many different ways. We shot over 36,000 feet of film in California and Minnesota. It takes 90 feet of film for a 60-second commercial and 45 feet for a 20-second commercial. It averaged out to $10,000 or $12,000 a shot, which is dirt cheap for the quality of the commercials. They are very, very top stuff, the best I've ever worked with. But everyone was very nervous about Georgia at the beginning. Safety, of course, was one of the big considerations, but it didn't end there. We didn't know how the public would react to seeing Earl around so many people. They might have preferred to see him alone."

The first commercial was to show young people restocking a stream with trout. Earl was to come splashing up the stream with Sasha at his side. He would help the young people throw the trout into the stream; then they would take a break and have a beer. The first take went perfectly. It was a sunny day, and the spray from the rushing stream sparkled for the cameras. Sasha loved the water and seemed unconcerned with the people. She frolicked at Earl's side, and the extras managed to smile for the cameras while keeping one eye on her.

However, during the second take, Sasha became interested in the trout. At first she tried to catch them with her feet, but then she realized they were coming from a central source. She bounded upstream directly toward the group who were flinging the trout into the water with a net. One man took the handle of his net and raised it up as if it were a club. Sasha reared back on her hind legs.

Earl thrust himself between the man and Sasha, and shouted "No." Sasha dropped to all fours; she made a few little playful moves in the water. Earl turned to the man who had raised the net instead of planting it in front of her as he had been taught. "Never, never threaten her. You'll get yourself hurt. She's much quicker and stronger than you, so you are never going to win in a challenge. If you feel you are in danger, plant your pole and take one or two steps back, always keeping the pole between you and her. Trust me that I always know where she is and what she is about to do. I have to be able to trust you to use your common sense."

Earl took Sasha for a swim, saying, "Come on, lover, I promised you a good time in the water today."

"I loved to hear Earl talk to Sasha," says Abby Costello. "It was strange. He went to a great deal of trouble to make it clear to us that she was a wild animal and couldn't be trusted, but he was incredibly gentle with her, and I really think that Sasha has a certain feeling for him. Even though there were many moments when it was clear that she wanted her own way, I never ever got the feeling that Earl was in trouble."

The next morning's call was at 6:30 for a commercial labeled Beaver Dam. The story behind this commercial was simple. Two young men were to canoe past a beaver dam. Earl was to be in the background clearing away some debris that had clogged a stream. Sasha would play at his side in the water. Earl was to spot the two young canoers, wave hello, and they would stop and have a beer together.

At dawn, a caravan of trucks and cars assembled to shoot this simple commercial. One truck had a canoe in it, and one had the man-made beaver dam of twigs and chicken wire. Earl's comment about the dam was, "No self-respecting beaver would go near it. Looks like the beaver equivalent of a cheap motel."

The commercial was to be filmed deep in the Sumpter National Forest off an unpaved road. Earl maneuvered his thirty-eight-foot trailer down the treacherous road. At the location spot, everyone was warned to watch out for rattlesnakes, which like to come out in the sunshine.

Ted Mapes of the American Humane Association perched on a rock in the shade, looking very elegant. A tall man in his late sixties who was once a stand-in for Jimmy Stewart and Gary Cooper, he was there to observe the filming for the Association, which asks to observe all films that use animals. The Association sponsors the Patsy awards, the animal kingdom's Oscars. The nominations are made by the Humane Association, and the public votes for the winner. Two years ago Sasha won a Patsy. Since Sasha is not seen on the east coast or in the mid-Atlantic states, the fact that she won a second prize in this national contest made Earl extremely proud.

After watching Earl work, Ted Mapes said, "I was impressed with the way Hammond handled the bear. He's obviously a man who knows his way around animals, and the relationship between man and bear is genuine." While Lear set up the cameras for the filming of the commercial about the beaver dam, Ted and Earl chatted about Ted's experience in Hollywood. Earl brought Sasha down to the river and tied her to a tree with a long rope so she could play in the water.

After a few hours, the cameras and beaver dams were ready. Earl untied Sasha and brought her in front of the cameras. While the crew and the extras paid little attention to her, the birds immediately started clattering, warning all animals in the vicinity that a dangerous animal was near. Sasha jumped into the water, and Earl yelled for someone to grab a log or bush for her to play with. He wanted to keep her occupied while Lear was shooting. Within minutes, Rod appeared carrying an entire tree on his shoulder. In his red jacket and peaked hat, he looked exactly like one of the seven dwarfs in a non-Disney version of Snow White.

Rod shoved the log into the water; it weighed close to a hundred pounds. Sasha stood between two boulders in the water and held the log upright with her front paws. She chewed on it as if it were a large twig. She was playing where one of the more dangerous white water canoeing scenes was shot in *Deliverance,* and someone asked Earl if there was any danger that she might be carried downstream. "Do you see any 800-pound boulders tumbling downstream?" Earl asked deadpan.

As soon as the canoe skimmed into her vision, Sasha bounded from her position between the boulders. Earl pivoted and yelled to the men in the canoe, "She's not going for *you,* she wants the canoe. Let her have it."

Then he started to laugh. He tried to run through the water to catch up to Sasha, but the current was so strong that he could only move very slowly.

Doug Coffin was one of the men in the canoe, and he bailed out headfirst. He was asked what Sasha looked like when she was going toward him. "That's a good question. I did a brief sketch, and then I typed up a few pages, but finally I realized that I had to leave the canoe, and I didn't want to get my sketch pad wet . . . I don't know what she looked like . . . she looked big!"

Sasha showed no interest in Doug as he scrambled to shore. When she got to the canoe, she lifted one enormous paw and put it on the front thwart, splintering it instantly. As she put more weight on the paw, the canoe sank into the water. Sasha got into the canoe and watched the water spill over the sides. She seemed mystified because it wasn't moving.

"She wants a ride," said Earl laughing. "She thinks it's our canoe at home, and she remembers the Minnesota shooting. She thinks canoes are the way bears *are supposed* to travel. Come on, baby, you've sunk it. It can't take you anywhere."

Sasha shook her head at him. "Pussycat, that canoe is sunk." Earl asked someone to get him a can of beer. "I'll give you a beer if you get out of the canoe." Earl poured the beer into Sasha's feed pan and put it on the shore. Sasha climbed out of the canoe and began licking up the beer in her feed pan. "It works every time. She loves beer."

The most complicated commercial was saved until the end when, presumably, everyone would be more relaxed working with Sasha. Called the Geese-banding Commercial, the storyboard pictured a small group of young people banding geese by the side of the river. Suddenly, Earl and Sasha come out through the woods. Earl comes over and helps one of the group put a band around a goose's leg. Then everyone opens up a cooler and has a beer.

Abby Costello was to play the amateur naturalist, and she and her husband, Tom, and Doug Coffin were each given a goose to hold. The geese were from Long Island and they had clipped wings, which is why they did not fly away at the sight of Sasha.

Earl's first fear was that Sasha's curiosity would make her want to play with the geese. His second fear was that the geese, which were very powerful animals, would struggle free from the actors' arms. He was not exactly sure what would happen in a free-for-all between Sasha and a goose, and he was worried about the people who might get caught between them. He had deliberately kept Sasha very hungry so that she would be eager to get to her feed pan when she heard Eddie banging it, but there were so many variables in this commercial that he was concerned.

When Lear called "Action!" Eddie began to bang the feed pan. He was hidden behind a beer cooler. To get to Eddie, Sasha had to walk right past Tom Costello and Doug Coffin. Each of them held a goose.

As Sasha ambled past Coffin, her attention was attracted by the flapping wings in his arms. Coffin had tried to calm the goose, but at the sight of Sasha it grew agitated. It took all of Coffin's strength to keep the goose in his arms. Sasha was no longer interested in her feed pan, but definitely curious about the goose. Coffin calmly took a step backward. From behind the cooler, Eddie lifted his voice, "Come on, baby doll . . . dinner is over here. It's not the goose." Sasha took another step toward Coffin. Earl was about to jump in between them when Sasha's attention returned to her feed pan. She walked past Coffin and crossed to the cooler. Lear yelled, "Cut!" and everybody breathed a sigh of relief.

"I was really proud of Doug Coffin in that scene," said Earl. "He was one of the ones who was most nervous in the beginning. To tell the truth, I wasn't sure how he'd react when the bear was loose, but he made all the right moves."

After shooting the scene, Earl put Sasha back into her cage. Lear needed shots of Abby, Tom, and Doug sharing a beer with Earl. These scenes are much tougher to film than they look. The actors have to pretend to be having a good time, while assistants are interrupting constantly to spray the beer cans so they glisten.

Earl felt awkward because he was not an actor and did not know how to behave before a camera. However, Abby thinks it can be harder for a trained actor to work in a commercial than for a person without acting experience. "Whatever emotion they want has to be immediately recognizable, a cliché. As an actor, you try for subtlety, and I always feel squeezed in and tightened down when I work in a commercial. But I was very impressed with the way Earl worked as an actor. I know he doesn't think of himself as one, but he really seems relaxed in front of the cameras. He wasn't afraid to suggest things to Lear. As I watched Earl work, I could be more spontaneous myself.

"We were supposed to be enjoying ourselves, but the reality was that someone was always whispering, 'Hold your can so the label shows.' But when Earl started telling stories and making everyone laugh, we really did begin to enjoy ourselves."

Over and over again, during the two-week filming, everyone talked about what a wonderful time they were having. Lear felt Earl had changed completely from the other times he had worked with him. "It was as if he had been through two years of successful analysis. The difference was astounding. I don't know whether it was because he had his own farm, or the fact that the commercials had been so successful, but I have never had a better time on a shooting."

The good feelings between people came across on the film. Despite the obvious phoniness of the situations, the young people who greet Earl and Sasha seem genuinely glad to see them. The chemistry between man and bear that made the commercials such a success in the first place appears to spark the whole group. In Los Angeles, when the commercial with the geese was tested for audience reaction, it received the highest score of any Hamm's commercial in history. A score of over 12 is considered very good, and advertising executives are overjoyed if a commercial scores between 16 and 18; but this commercial scored a 23 on the Burke test.

"It wasn't just that we all had a good time," explains Tom Costello, having heard about the success of the commercials. "It was a wonderful feeling of shared responsibility. We felt we wanted to give our all for Earl. Nobody trusted the bear, but we did trust him, and we felt a certain obligation not to let him down."

Abby Costello says, "When I found out there was always a gun on the set, I began to understand how much was at stake. Earl loves that bear, and it's got nothing to do with the money. He's as close as you can get to an animal. Everyone felt a responsibility not to put her in jeopardy. I think we all had a great deal of respect for their friendship. After all, a bear is a bear. How many bears do you have as friends in a lifetime?"

13

Mommy, Mommy, Mignon's Coming

Liz was in her ninth month of pregnancy. She and Earl had decided to have the baby at the farm and had arranged for a doctor and a nurse to come to the house. As Liz's due date grew near, it became almost impossible for her to walk Mignon without help. "I was much larger than I had been with either Niki or Jenny. I felt as if I weighed a ton and a half, and Mignon *actually* weighed a ton and a half."

One particularly cold March afternoon, Liz was exhausted. She had been up at six, getting Niki and Jenny off to school. Missy told her she would take Mignon out for a walk alone. Gratefully, Liz collapsed on her bed and went to sleep.

Missy escorted Mignon up from the basement without incident. Outside, Mignon walked slowly, picking up loose chunks of ice and putting them in her mouth. The air was damp, the sky gray and overcast.

They headed out past the chicken coop where several chickens had been slaughtered recently. As Mignon approached the coop, she started to veer away from Missy, who quickly uncovered a baby bottle of warm milk she was carrying under her coat. Usually the sight of a bottle kept Mignon close, but now she ignored the bottle and began to walk in nervous little circles. Suddenly her ears flipped forward, her tail stiffened, and her trunk curled up under her mouth in a charge position. She gave one loud trumpet and headed back to the house at a run.

Missy turned and ran after her, yelling, "Stop! Stop!" She had no idea what had caused Mignon to panic. Mignon slipped and slid on the ice, gathering speed on the slight decline toward the back door. Somehow, Missy managed to outrun her and skitted toward the house. Still yelling at Mignon to stop, Missy spread her arms wide, planting her back to the door.

"I don't know how I expected to stop her," said Missy afterward, "and I'll never understand what happened next. It was a feat worthy of Houdini. Without even stepping on my toe, she got past me and crashed through the back door, toppling it to the floor as if it were paper. One minute she was outside, and the next minute she was inside.

Jenny was the first to see Mignon running through the kitchen toward the living room. "Mommy, Mommy, Mignon's coming," she shouted. Luckily, Jenny's voice woke Liz. She stumbled out of bed and opened her bedroom door. Mignon trembled before Liz, her head butting into Liz's extended stomach. Still having no idea what Mignon was doing in the living room, Liz stroked Mignon rhythmically and wrapped her arms as far around her as they could reach.

Earl heard the shouting and came running up from the barn. "I just assumed she was starting labor. It never occurred to me that the noise could be anything else. I was already cursing the fact that it was such a cold, overcast day and the roads were icy."

When he rushed into the living room and saw Mignon there, his first words were, "Goddamn it, Liz. When are you going to stop being Mommy and remember she's an elephant."

By this time, Mignon had calmed down. Liz sat cross-legged by Mignon's head, holding her trunk and letting her suck her thumb. Missy explained that she had been out by the chicken coop with Mignon when suddenly Mignon spooked and bolted for the house.

"It must have been the chicken blood that scared her," said Liz. "If Jenny hadn't woke me up, I think we might have lost our bedroom door."

"She was heading for the bed," said Earl, shaking his head. "One night we're going to be sleeping and that goddamn elephant is going to come through the house and hide under the bed." Earl sank into a big easy chair and lit a cigarette. Jenny came and sat in his lap.

"I wonder what would have happened if I hadn't woken up?" says Liz, laughing.

"You mean to tell me you couldn't hear an elephant coming through the house? You can hear the tiniest cry of Niki or Jenny, but you can't hear an elephant?" said Earl.

Self-righteously Liz reminded Earl that elephants' feet are padded and that there are hundreds of circus stories about elephants sneaking through the camp at night and stealing liquor or candy.

A few weeks later, visiting friends commented on the broken door patched with corrugated tin. As everyone sat around the kitchen table drinking coffee, Liz began to have labor pains.

"They were so mild I didn't pay too much attention. Our friends left around five in the afternoon, and I told Earl he had better call Dr. Richards and his nurse. I was filthy dirty so I took a shower. Around 7:30 in the evening, I went into pretty heavy labor. Even though the doctor had been to the farm before, he got lost. The nurse made it before he did. When the doctor arrived, the contractions were coming every few minutes. He said it would be a few hours, so he headed straight for the barn and the cellar to visit the animals. He had seen lots of births, but had few chances to be close to an elephant. Luckily, he did leave Mignon in time to be there at the birth. We had a baby girl, Vanessa, and Earl was wonderful the whole time."

A few days later, Liz showed Vanessa to Mignon. "I had had fantasies about what cute sisters they would make. Mignon loved babies. She would make a bee-line for baby carriages and strollers, and she was always gentle with them. Yet when she saw Vanessa, she tried to pretend she didn't exist. She didn't sniff at her or anything. Even now that Vanessa is over a year old she doesn't want to have anything to do with her."

In early June, Earl and Liz took Mignon for a walk. Liz carried Vanessa, now three months old, in a baby tote strapped to her chest. The hills of the pasture were dotted with daisies, buttercups, and paint-brushes. Liz and Earl sat in the sun with Vanessa lying on a blanket between them. Vanessa grabbed Earl's finger and wouldn't let go. Earl looked up at Mignon in the distance, then turned to Liz. "Remember when I bought you a diamond the first year we were together? You had a fit—you said that if I bought you a diamond, why couldn't I get you an elephant?"

Liz laughed. "It's beautiful. Some day I'll have to start wearing it. It has three flaws, and the light bounces off them. You told me it was to remind me that I'm not perfect."

Mignon had turned and was running back through the pasture to them. "Now that I'm approaching forty, I appreciate diamonds. You don't have to worry about them running through the house and busting doors."

Mignon stopped in front of them. She started to lower her body so she could lie next to Liz. "Careful, careful. . . . We've got a new baby here." Mignon rolled on her side and waved her trunk in Liz's face. Liz grabbed it and blew a kiss down it.

"Yummy. You've been eating wild strawberries—that's delicious."

Suddenly Liz looked over at Earl. "On the other hand, if we had never had Mignon, I would never have known what strawberry-flavored elephant kisses tasted like."